The Boy in the Lake

Also by Eric Swanson

The Greenhouse Effect

The Boy in the Lake

Eric Swanson

St. Martin's Griffin New York

Design by James Sinclair

Library of Congress Cataloging-in-Publication Data

Swanson, Eric.
The boy in the lake : a novel / Eric Swanson.
p. cm.
ISBN 0-312-20281-4 (hc)
ISBN 0-312-26297-3 (pbk)
I. Title
PS3569.W2685B69 1999
813'.54—dc21 99-20094
CIP

First St. Martin's Griffin Edition: May 2000

10 9 8 7 6 5 4 3 2 1

This book is for Bob Dombroski
and for
Julia Stando Kuntz

Tattoos

When I was small, my grandmother told me stories. One of my favorites was about the medallion she wore around her neck: a wafer of thin gold with a picture of a saint on one side and a circle of strange-looking letters engraved on the other. She told me that her mother had put the medallion around her neck the day she left Poland to come to America. The letters, she explained, were Polish. They formed a prayer that she promised to teach me when I was old enough to need it. Until then, I didn't have to worry because God looked after little children.

I was ten years old when I learned that the story behind the medallion wasn't necessarily true. Another version existed, which I heard one night at the Polish Club, where my grandmother went to play rummy on Saturdays. The players—several cadaverous men and two old women—met in the club's basement. I waited in the upstairs lounge. The wooden folding chairs were apt to snap shut if you weren't careful, but ginger ale was only five cents a glass and I liked seeing the adults get weepy and red-faced as they sang mournful folk songs to each other across the rickety tables in a language I didn't understand.

One Saturday, an old woman sat down across from me and offered me a cookie. Though she introduced herself as an old friend of my grandmother's, I declined her offer—in part because she had a hairy patch the size of my hand on her cheek, and in part because the cookie was the round kind with a clot of poisonously red jelly in the center. These two things together gave me a bad feeling.

After asking me a few questions about myself—my age, my height, my favorite foods, and, inexplicably, whether I was interested in rocket ships—she told me my grandmother was one of the bravest women she knew, and that she didn't think she'd have been able to do the same things if she'd been in her shoes. When I asked her what shoes she meant—imagining her trying to stuff her fat feet into my grandmother's tiny orthopedic slippers—she laughed, which made the hairy patch on her cheek quiver like some sort of terrified small animal.

She went on to explain that the Germans had attacked my grandmother's village back at the beginning of World War II. My grandmother had hidden in the woods and watched her family and friends picked off one by one, like squirrels. Women raped while they bled to death, men strung up in trees with their bellies slit open, their guts spilling to the ground. When the soldiers left, she slipped back into the village and gathered up whatever food and bits of money the Germans had left behind, then traveled alone across the border into Czechoslovakia, on foot.

The medallion engraved with the picture of a saint had come from a neighbor's corpse.

Though some of what the old woman told me sailed over my head, the bloodier images made a deep and rather terrifying impression, like the gruesome bits of old fairy tales. I made a conscious decision to believe that she'd invented the story of the attack on my grandmother's village and her subsequent theft of the medallion. Perhaps, I reasoned, she'd wanted to punish me for not taking the cookie she'd offered. Perhaps she'd seen through my politeness and knew I thought she was ugly.

For a long time afterward, I remained proud of my decision. I felt as though I had earned my place in the ranks of adulthood. Obviously, if two stories contradicted each other, one had to be true and the other false.

Now, of course, I can juggle several variations of a single story without confusion. It's a professional skill, a habit derived from listening to people who come to me for therapeutic help. They tell their stories over and over again, trying to will order upon the myriad hurts, large and small, that form the texture of their lives. Details left out of one version almost always show up in another. Slowly, over time, a gap almost always reveals itself, a null space where different versions of the same story fail to overlap.

I believe this is where the truth lives. Not in any particular telling, but in the gaps, the silences between.

Stephen Porter, a patient of mine for a little over six months, had had a gift for silence.

He'd been referred to me by M. J. Sweeney, one of my colleagues at a teaching hospital where I'd worked when I first came to New York. M. J. had a fairly direct way of speaking—*blunt* I suppose, is probably the better word—and when she called to talk to me about Stephen, she said straight out that I was right for him because of my history. It didn't occur to me until after I'd hung up the phone that she'd probably used the word in its clinical, rather than its social, sense.

Stephen was late for our first session, which didn't seem the most auspicious of beginnings. When he finally came slouching through the door to my office, I thought immediately of a starved rabbit. He was extremely thin, with nearly white eyebrows and eyelashes, common enough among people with red hair. He was tall, though, and broad around the shoulders, and I guessed that in a few years he'd probably fill out. A faint red stubble defined his chin and upper lip. He was sixteen years old.

He sat down without saying hello, curling his body against one arm of the couch. I was distracted for the first few minutes, wondering whether to tell him it wasn't the best of all places for him to put his weight. The couch had begun to creak whenever someone sat down too hard in certain spots. When I finally mentioned it however, he didn't move. In fact, he didn't acknowledge me at all.

"Feel free to say anything you want," I continued, trying to avoid sounding too hearty.

He sat silently, his expression halfway between petulant and stony. I felt almost grateful when the radiator started clanging. Every time I'd call about it, the superintendent would tell me that the problem wasn't the radiator but the boiler. *It's old,* he'd say, *an old building*. If I mentioned that the rent miraculously managed to keep pace with the times, he suddenly lost his command of English and conveniently reverted to some sort of incomprehensible pidgin tongue. I'd thought about moving, but my office is only four blocks from my apartment: east-west blocks, which are longer than north-south ones, but it's still a convenient walk.

Stephen glanced at the radiator and then went back to staring at his knees.

"I'm trying to get that fixed," I explained. "I'm sorry. Do you have any questions?"

He mumbled something.

"I didn't catch that."

"They usually ask me the questions," he said, louder.

"Well we can do things differently."

"They say that, too. The other doctors."

"Well I'm not a doctor, for starters."

He peeled a piece of skin off his thumb with his fingernail.

"What are you then?"

"Technically, I'm an MSW. Master of Social Work."

"What's the difference?"

"I can't prescribe medication, for one thing."

He looked up then, the first sign of feeling he'd shown. "What if I need more pills?"

"You can always see Dr. Sweeney at the hospital."

After a minute, he looked back down in his lap and methodically picked a scab off the back of his hand. There wasn't any blood, but he wiped his hand on the couch cushion anyway. Then he looked across the room at me and smiled briefly, a saint in agony.

"Guess I don't rate the big guns no more," he said.

I couldn't say for sure whether he meant the remark as an insult. In fact, I never learned as much about him as I hoped I would. After six months, he simply stopped coming. The last I heard of him was in a news item that appeared recently in the back of the Metro section of the *New York Times*.

The article was a single paragraph long. Apart from Stephen's name and age, it mentioned only that the cuts on his wrists had been self-inflicted and that the bar behind which he'd been found was a known meeting place for gay men.

About a week after Stephen's suicide, my grandmother died, so unobtrusively that her exit from this world went unremarked for nearly a week before a concerned neighbor discovered the body. To die at home, under clean sheets and dressed in a nearly new nightgown, was perfectly consistent with my grandmother's entire approach to life: she couldn't tolerate messes. Unfortunately, the neighbor who found her was unable to appreciate such niceties. Even in the middle of winter, in a barely heated bedroom, a certain amount of physical decomposition had taken place.

I don't like to think about this.

The county coroner determined that my grandmother had died of a heart attack; a quick, fairly tidy way to die. He placed the time of her death somewhere between nine and eleven in the evening on Valentine's Day, thus squaring my grandmother's habitual neatness with an unsuspected gift for irony.

These two deaths, my grandmother's and Stephen's, have made me uncomfortably aware of the fragility of the human vessel. They have also called attention to the fact that no matter how tidy people may be, they always leave something of a mess behind when they die. There are houses to clean out and worldly goods to give away, to say nothing of all the sentiments left dangling like so many snapped clotheslines.

A certain snobbishness had kept me away from home for more than twenty-five years. If my grandmother alone had died, I'm not sure I'd have returned. I'm indebted to Stephen, actually, for making up my mind to return to Ohio and clean up all the loose ends that had gathered in my absence.

There's probably no way to entirely escape regret at the moment of death. Still, when my time comes I'd at least like to know that I'd left as little mess as possible behind.

Amity is hardly the sunny, flat farmland people typically imagine when they think of Ohio. Situated more or less diagonally across the river from Wheeling, West Virginia, it's a town in name only: There aren't enough residents to actually merit a charter. Its public institutions consist of a Catholic church, a post office, a two-pump filling station, and a bar.

There are also two schools, a public one and a Catholic one. I went to the public school first, then to the Catholic school. After my parents died, I left Amity altogether to live with an aunt and uncle in Columbus—which seemed to me, at thirteen, a far more sophisticated place, replete with sidewalks, strip malls, and movie theaters.

Amity is mining country, a twisted landscape, spotted with rickety houses still standing a hundred years after the mining companies had thrown them up for all the men who thought digging coal would make them rich.

My grandfather had been one of those men. He'd emigrated from Eastern Europe with my grandmother at the beginning of the Second World War. He died in a mine collapse a few years before I was born. My father, their only child, also worked in the mines; but by the late 1950s the seams had started going dry and steady jobs were growing scarce. So even after he got married, he and my mother lived in my grandmother's house, ostensibly to save money until they could afford a place of their own.

My father skulked around the house like someone whose dearest wish was to become invisible. My mother actually succeeded in vanishing, dissolving herself nightly in a bottle of scotch or bourbon or, failing more palatable solutions, Listerine. She disappeared piece by piece, like the Cheshire Cat; except in her case the last piece to go wasn't her smile but her eyes—also like a cat's, wily and full of secrets.

Memories of my parents laughing together or smiling flutter by too quickly, like dry leaves. A picnic where they lean together under an enormous tree. A party where a man on the radio has just announced that someone young and Irish like my mother is now president. On a beach, my mother's long fingers rubbing suntan oil on the ropy muscles of my father's back. One day, my father came home with jugs of water, which he carried down to the basement. My mother and grandmother carried down boxes of instant milk and cans of green beans, corn, and carrots. This urgent accumulation of imperishables had something to do with pigs and an island near Florida, which in 1962 I knew principally as the state shaped like a lady's leg. A few days later, my parents brought the cans and the boxes back upstairs and my father hoisted me in his arms high up in the air. My mother, laughing, told him to watch out or I'd get sick all over.

Around my fourth birthday, my mother swelled up like an egg. My father would lay his hand on the print cotton blouse stretched tight against her stomach, and my little brother or sister who was making her swell would suddenly kick from inside her stomach, making my father's hand jump. Sometimes when it kicked I thought I could see the outline of a tiny foot. Then one day, it kicked too hard and blood seeped out onto the kitchen floor, pooling under the chair where my mother sat trying to hold the baby inside until my father came back with the truck to take her across the river to the Wheeling hospital. Her face turned the color of old paper and her lips were white, pressed tightly together. Blood oozed past her fingers.

She stayed in the hospital for several days, and when she came back, pale and quiet, she went immediately to her bedroom at the end of the hall. She didn't bring home a little brother or sister as she was supposed to, and I was instructed very carefully not to ask any questions. I was told, in fact, to act as if the whole thing had never happened: the swelling, the kicking, the blood on the kitchen floor.

For a while, a lot of the women in the neighborhood came by to visit. They spent hours in the bedroom where my mother lay propped up by pillows, and when the bedroom door opened I could hear her voice murmuring, *You're so kind.*

When at last she emerged from the bedroom, we had a new president, an older one who wasn't Irish. There were dark circles under my mother's eyes, and her hair stuck to her temples. Though she often had a highball before and after dinner, she rarely laughed or smiled. Those parts of her had already begun to disappear.

While my mother was recovering from her miscarriage, my grandmother and I started taking long walks together. Her house sat at the bottom of a tall hill, at the top of which stood an old farmhouse and a dilapidated barn surroundted by rail fence. A few thin, scabby cows grazed in the field around the barn.

The farmer who owned them was an old man with deep cuts in his face, under his eyes, and along his cheeks. One of the cuts was his mouth. Whenever we saw him out in the yard, my grandmother and I would pass by quickly, looking neither right nor left. If he wasn't there, we'd stop at the rail fence to say hello to the cows.

"We had cows," my grandmother told me one morning. "Back in Poland." I thought that's what she said, at any rate. Her English wasn't always clear. For the sake of clarity I asked her if she brought her cows with her.

"Good grief," she replied, "what a question."

I insisted though, because the whole matter of possessions had recently begun to assume great importance to me. I'd started to collect things in a copper tin under my bed. So far, I'd assembled a green and yellow marble found in the church parking lot, some feathers, and three gold stars my cousin Judith had given me. I hadn't formulated a specific plan for these items; I kept them just in case. They were my things.

"No," my grandmother said finally, after a few moments. "I didn't."

"Why not?"

"The war."

When I asked her what war was, she turned away to stare across the old farmer's weedy field. I listened for a while to a distant sound like the rattling of tin cans. After a few minutes, one of the cows wandered up to the fence.

"Don't get too close," my grandmother warned. "Cow'll bite your fingers right off."

Past the barn, on the other side of the hill, was a meadow, where giant stalks of goldenrod grew, and countless daisies, and tiger lilies broad as my hand. On hot, summer days, the acrid smell of parched weeds clung to our arms and legs, and the dry grass rang with the hollow shrill of crickets. Some of the paths through the meadow led to a shallow creek, some to the road across from the school I would attend in the not-so-distant future. Others led to secret rooms of flat grass, hidden behind walls of weeds.

My grandmother and I usually took the same path down to the creek—the way, she told me, that my grandfather used to walk before he *passed*. That's the word she used, which made me think he'd simply gotten lost while out walking one day, and passed right out of town. I liked the open-endedness of this image, the sense of people going on and on, their paths sometimes crossing, sometimes not. It came as a shock later on, therefore, when my mother told me he'd been crushed in a mine collapse.

On nice days, my grandmother and I spent an hour or so sitting by the creek that ran through the meadow. She sat on a pair of stones along the bank while I looked for things to put in my copper box. Pine cones, leaves, pieces of colored glass I thought were jewels. Once, I discovered a broken bird's egg. The shell was soft, like warm leather, and coated with brown slime. My grandmother made me throw it in the water, and for an entire week afterward I made plans to go back at night and find it again. For several nights running, I dreamed I was a bird.

When I was finished exploring, I would sit beside my grandmother and she would tell me stories. Sometimes it was obvious these stories were about herself, when she was a little girl. Other times, I had to figure it out on my own.

"There were two boys," she began one day, "and three girls. Eva, Sophie, and Julka. The three girls all slept in the same bed, and the two boys in another. In the winters, it was so cold they put the mattresses by the potbellied stove and slept there, the whole family, even their mother and father. They were rich, because they had a potbellied stove."

She told how this girl, Julka, had taken a steamer across the ocean to America. At five years old, of course, I had no idea what a steamer was and I'd yet to see the ocean—though I had ridden in a boat around the Lake Erie, which made me sick. Apprehensively, I asked if the girl named Julka ever thought about going back across the ocean. I was enormously relieved when my grandmother told me no.

"Not even to see her brothers and sisters?"

"They passed," my grandmother replied. "In the war."

The airport closest to my grandmother's house is more than 100 miles away in Columbus. As soon as I collect my luggage, I head over to the Avis rental desk where the girl behind the counter scrutinizes my driver's license as though it might be fake. I wonder if I've aged that much since the photo was taken. The girl at the Avis counter seems vastly younger than I am, a category that includes far too many people nowadays. She wears her greenish-blond hair teased out along the back and the sides, and appears to have expended a good deal of time applying blue eye shadow to each lid and the surrounding area.

"Christian Fowler," she says, handing back my license. "Is that a German name?"

"Czechoslovakian," I reply.

"Don't sound like that to me."

I'm not sure if she's making conversation or looking for something suspicious. I put on my charming face, the one I use for bank tellers and cashiers.

"The way I heard it," I tell her, "the fellow at immigration couldn't understand my grandfather's name, so he spelled it the best way he could."

"Well, that don't seem right to me," the girl says somewhat petulantly. "Seems to me," she adds, "a person should at least be able to keep their own *name*." She squints down at her terminal screen. "You'll be taking the car two weeks?"

"That's right."

She types more information into her terminal. The printer spits out a piece of paper, which she passes across the counter for me to sign where she's circled.

"Business or pleasure?" she asks.

"Beg pardon?"

"I just wondered you come to Columbus for business or pleasure."

"Ah. Neither, actually."

She presses her hands together on the counter in something like a prayer position, and arranges her face in an attitude of engaged interest. I hand her back the contract.

"Really, I'm just visiting."

"*Oh-h-h,*" she replies, lowering her voice. "You wouldn't be a private detective or something?"

To my left, a pair of automated glass doors slides open and shut, admitting a rush of preternaturally freezing air that feels almost solid, like a piece of the night sky. I tell the girl she must be an excellent judge of character.

"It weren't but a guess," she says.

"Some people are better at guessing than others."

"Oh, I don't know."

"No, truly. You have a gift. You should appreciate it."

The girl blushes, and hands me the keys and my copy of the rental agreement in such a way that our fingers touch. I pull back quickly and ask if she has a map.

"You'll be okay driving at night won't you?" she asks.

"Hope so."

"Supposed to snow again."

"I'd better get going then."

"You take care."

As I turn away, she calls out. "Say!" Now she's leaning almost all the way over her counter, hissing at me in a stage whisper. "What kind of case is it?"

I stare blankly until I remember the white lie I told, then shake my head. "I can't really tell you now, can I?"

"Confidential, huh?"

I hope it looks like I'm weighing my response as I try to come up with a plausible reply.

"Something like that."

Which is close enough to the truth that I don't feel bad walking away. I'm not sure if the person I'm looking for is still alive, after all, or living in the place I think he might be.

The flat, hopeful voice of the girl behind the rental counter follows me, thanking me for choosing Avis.

It sounds like an accusation.

My rental car is easy enough to find in the parking lot. I let it idle a few minutes before heading onto the interstate. Already the snow has begun to fall rather heavily and traffic moves at a crawl. Thick, damp flakes swarm across my windshield, as the wipers trace twin fans across the glass, producing a weirdly bifurcated view of the nighttime scenery. The small cities of Zanesville and Cambridge appear one after another, two bright islands shining in a sprawling dark broken occasionally by the fluorescent gleam of a truck stop.

Along the way, I pass an old red pickup truck with four people sitting tightly together in the cab: my father, my mother, my grandmother, and myself. We're on our way back from Columbus after visiting my mother's brother, Uncle Ames. My mother has two brothers, Uncle Patrick and Uncle Ames. Uncle Patrick lives in town, and teaches English at the local high school. Uncle Ames lives in Columbus, where he owns a funeral parlor. We visit him once a month, or sometimes every other month.

Before each trip, my mother spreads a blanket on the seat to keep the packing off our good clothes. I sit next to my father, and when I'm tired of watching the road I study his hands, which are huge and heavy, like blocks of stone. In fact, everything about my father is outsized. He's well over six feet tall, so that when he drives the steering wheel grazes his knees. His wide bony forehead slopes down over his eyes. He rumbles, rather than speaks.

Sometimes, when he shifts gears, he drops a hand on my knee and gives a surprise squeeze. Taking her cue from him, my grandmother—sitting on the other side of me—squeezes my other knee. I wriggle between them, laughing and squealing, arching against the back of the seat.

"Judas priest!" my mother hisses, tense and miserable, pressed against the passenger side door. "Will you stop that *caterwauling*?"

She uses words that nobody else would use, culled from the vocabulary exercises in the *Reader's Digest* magazines that she steals from the Wheeling Public Library. Though she insists she's not stealing, but only *pinching* them. She smiles at the puzzled look my father sometimes gives whenever she throws out more obscure terms, like *cerebrate* or *preponderance.*

"Life among the *Neanderthals* is so charming," she murmurs in response to his perplexity, sipping her highball, which isn't really a highball but a *palliative.* My father rarely answers her taunts. He rarely responds to her at all, in fact. He doesn't have to, since the atmosphere between them speaks volumes. Tensed and charged, like the air before a thunderstorm.

My mother fusses the whole way to Columbus, squinting in the side mirror, fixing her skirt, fiddling with the radio stations. Now a report on the Gemini astronauts, now something about the troops in Hanoi. If my father complains about her switching stations so often, she tells him, "It's terribly important to keep up with current events," pronouncing the word as if describing potential damage: *tear-ably.*

The drive takes nearly two hours. Uncle Ames and Aunt Jane live in a four-bedroom house in a suburb where all the streets look like rows of polished teeth. Every room is immaculate, and carefully planned. In the living room, for instance, the pale yellow sofa and cream-colored chairs match the colors on the walls and curtains, and the pastel drawings of flowers in round frames. We never sit in the living room when we visit, though. We sit in the den instead, a smaller room with paneled walls and a dark carpet. Uncle Ames mixes drinks in a silver shaker behind the bar, then carries them on a tray to my mother and Aunt Jane, who sit together on a love seat.

They sit like the ladies in the Sears catalogue, with their legs crossed at the knees and faces smiling like they've just chewed aspirin. When they lean toward each other to say hello or good-bye, they kiss the air.

Sometimes we sit in the kitchen, which doesn't smell of onions or cabbage, as my grandmother's kitchen does. Aunt Jane's kitchen is permeated by a vaguely chemical odor, a residue apparently left by her *woman.* At first, I think the term refers to some sort of female homunculus. Or perhaps a ghost. Only gradually, after listening to adult conversations, am I able to put together that her *woman* is someone who comes once a week to clean the house. Which gives Aunt Jane all the time she needs to take care of her wigs. My mother once observed in private that Aunt Jane has more wigs than any woman east of the Mississippi.

Nobody comes to help my grandmother clean her house. There aren't as many rooms, of course, and they're all small, crammed with furniture that doesn't match. In my grandmother's bedroom, you have to walk sideways between the dresser and the bed. The sun has bleached spots on the parlor rug. The kitchen cupboards are spotted and streaked with white where water has ruined the wood.

On our way back from Columbus, we'd sometimes pull into a truck stop for dinner. My father and I ordered hamburgers, which were served dripping with grease, and french fries so bloated they fell apart in our mouths. My mother usually ordered Jell-O salad. My grandmother had either tuna fish on a bun or fish sticks.

As soon as we ordered, I would excuse myself to the bathroom, where I'd while away a quarter of an hour flushing small objects down the toilets: pennies, packs of Heinz catsup or Domino sugar, stones from the parking lot. The roar and swish of the water as it swallowed my humble offerings seemed to satisfy some basic need. I was never allowed to flush the toilet over and over like that at home.

From time to time, truck drivers would shuffle in from the dining room and belly up to the urinals. The tattoos on their arms transfixed me: green snakes, women's breasts, Jesus with his heart exposed. I'd stare at the tattoos until the drivers caught me looking, at which point I felt I could ask them where they got their marks, and why, and if it had hurt when the needles pierced their skin.

Once, when I was five years old, a driver younger than most hoisted me up on the edge of one of the sinks so I could see his tattoo better. He had blue-black curly hair and an enormous set of straight white teeth. His skin was darker than mine, and slightly oily. He reminded me a of a comic book pirate. A blue bolt of lightning had been inked on his bicep, and when he flexed his arm the lightning bolt jumped a little.

Boldly, I asked if I could touch the tattoo.

"Sure, Spike," he replied, in a voice just above a whisper.

At first, I only tapped the bolt of lightning with my fingernail.

"My name's not Spike," I informed him.

"What is it then?"

I told him, Christian.

"You can do better than that, Chris," he said.

Using just my fingertip I traced the lightning bolt on his arm, and when I reached the sharp end he suddenly flexed his bicep and made the tattoo jump. We both laughed at that, and he moved an inch or two closer to me. He brought both his hands down to rest delicately on my knees, and tiny bumps appeared on his arms: gooseflesh.

"You're a little monkey," he said.

Just then, the bathroom door swung open and my father entered the room, calling my name. He stopped moving as soon as he saw what was going on, and the door swung back and forth behind him in a diminishing arc, until finally it stopped swinging altogether. My father held his ground, staring, as the truck driver straightened and stepped away in one slow, fluid movement, like a cat.

"He has a tattoo," I announced brightly.

Neither my father nor the driver said anything. My father simply stepped forward and swung me down from the sink, his eyes glazed and sad, his mouth pressed shut. He propelled me out of the bathroom, gripping my arm too tightly as we headed back through the dining room to our table.

"Don't ever, ever do that again," he said, in a choked, ragged voice that sounded like tires on gravel.

For several months after this incident, I would practice making tattoos on my arm; first using a pencil and then a pin from the tomato-shaped cushion in my grandmother's mending basket. Only once did I actually manage to stick myself hard enough to draw blood: a tiny crimson pearl I smeared with my finger and then tasted, which went a long way toward satisfying my curiosity. My interest was more practical than mystical, after all. I simply wanted to know what pins felt like, and how blood tasted, whether having lightning on one's arm would hurt.

When she first told me about Stephen, M. J. had mentioned only that we shared a few background similarities. She promised to messenger his file, and it was in my office by the end of the day.

The notes were precise, the handwriting surprisingly clear. Reading over the file I wondered whether someone who didn't know M. J. at all might conjure from her style an image of someone brisk, blond, and excruciatingly efficient—good with horses, maybe, and fond of tennis. In fact, M. J. is short and round, and dyes her hair a shade of red that looks best on new pennies. Visits to her office tend to inspire a type of fear that borders on awe. Something wild and unpleasant surely lives among the random mounds of books and journals sprawled across the floor, or in the trash can overflowing with empty take-out containers, balled up papers, and torn panty hose.

From the file, I learned that Stephen had come from the Midwest—though I considered Oklahoma a bit farther afield than Ohio. The religious element in his background was also somewhat stronger than mine: His father was in no way connected to the Catholic Church, but served as an evangelical minister in a Protestant denomination I had never heard of. His mother had no formal occupation. Aside from looking after her five children—of which Stephen was the youngest—she assisted her husband by visiting the sick, counseling women and young girls, and "witnessing" at Sunday services.

The Porters had moved to New York in 1987, to serve the Lord in Washington Heights, at the northern tip of Manhattan. Though Stephen was only five years old at the time, both parents reported that he'd adjusted smoothly, socialized well, and performed adequately at school. They could only confess shock when he swallowed a bottle of secobarbital just two days before his sixteenth birthday.

He'd had his stomach pumped in the emergency room, then he was sent up to the psych unit. During the initial consultation, he told M. J. that *they* had told him to take the pills. She couldn't get him to say who *they* were, and after a few more questions he stopped saying anything at all. So she admitted him for observation and prescribed chlorpromazine, 100 milligrams, twice a day.

There's always a chance that a strong antipsychotic medication might aggravate depression, but as far as antipsychotic treatments go, chlorpromazine is at least better than the old methods. In the early days of psychiatric medicine, psychotics were dropped down wells or injected with horse serum. Not too long ago, some psychiatrists advised pulling a patient's teeth as a cure for schizophrenia.

In a preliminary interview, Reverend and Mrs. Porter told M. J. that they had no idea how their son had gotten hold of the secobarbital. Apparently, neither of them thought very highly of modern medicine, which included all forms of prescription medication. Reverend Porter explained his position simply, saying that the Lord carried each soul in the palm of His hand. Naturally, M. J. asked why—in that case—they had brought Stephen to the hospital.

"It was my idea," his mother had replied. "My faith wandered."

Shortly after my first session with Stephen, Mrs. Porter called and asked if she could see me. She called on a Friday, and we made an appointment for the following Tuesday. She came without her husband, which may have accounted for the look of bewilderment on her face. I wondered how long it had been since she'd found herself alone in a room with a strange man.

She was a small woman. Sitting perfectly erect on the couch, she looked almost like a doll—or like a very young girl putting on her best company manners. I'd expected someone more drab, as if having faith necessarily rendered a person homely. A feather of pale hair trailed down her neck and faint red creases showed around her nose. She carried a plain white handkerchief in one hand.

She apologized for the handkerchief, saying she had a cold.

"You probably think my husband and I are terrible parents," she said, after a minute. "To raise a child so unhappy he would want to take his own life."

I sat forward in my chair and leaned my elbows on my knees. The urge to protect her felt genuine enough. I told her that children often felt overwhelmed by problems completely unrelated to their lives at home: pressures at school, traumas they might feel ashamed or unwilling to discuss, even some sort of chemical imbalance may lie at the root of their unhappiness.

She smiled, as if to thank me, and at the same time to let me know I didn't need to spare her.

"It's not easy to live in the shadow of a great man," she said.

"Your husband?"

She nodded.

"Holland was called when he was eight years old. There was an accident on his family's farm. One of the farm hands was hurt and his father told him to run to the house and call a doctor. Holland didn't move, he just stood there staring at the blood, the pained face of the man that had only been hired that day. He was a stranger, Mr. Fowler, there was no other connection.

"His father told him again to run to the house, but Holland—even now he can hardly say what happened. The closest he can come to describing it is that he came awake in this world. Which his father misunderstood as some sort of shock, and took him by the shoulders to force him back to the house. And received a shock of his own when Holland pushed him away. He disobeyed his father, you see. He went over to the hired man and laid his hands on his leg, and the blood ceased flowing."

Her story unnerved me in a way I found difficult to explain. Perhaps it was the complacent tone in which she told it. Several impulses plucked at me at once.

"I'm not exactly sure what you mean by *called*," I said finally. "Did he hear anything—a voice, voices?"

"No." Mrs. Porter tilted her head slightly, and offered another sad smile. "Are you a religious man, Mr. Fowler?"

With a patient, I'd look for the reason for asking: Curiosity usually reflects some sort of conflict about the issue at hand. But Mrs. Porter wasn't my patient. Accordingly, I replied that while I had respect for people's beliefs, I didn't hold any myself.

"Do you believe in the soul?" she asked.

"In the abstract or particular?"

She smiled more broadly then, apparently seeing through my evasion.

"And the Lord God formed man of the dust of the ground," she said, *"and breathed into his nostrils the breath of life; and man became a living soul."*

She closed her eyes momentarily and opened them again.

"My husband saw the hired man's soul, Mr. Fowler. Which was all the more exalting given the belief, common to some parts, that a black man could not possess one."

"Has he performed many healings since that time?"

"Just the one. Though he has never told me, I believe it torments him."

"I imagine it would."

She straightened, folding her hands in her lap.

"Not for the reasons you think."

The slim smile that flickered on her lips seemed to waver somewhere between seduction and pity. A glimmer of something carnal, like light glancing through a chink in a rock.

"Oh?" I managed.

"Not because he's failed. He doesn't believe he's being punished because he can't stop a wound from bleeding or remove a cancer. He takes his limits as his humility. But he still *sees*. He sees suffering where it originates, and he's powerless to stop those wounds."

"He has his vocation," I replied. "His church."

"He's a fine speaker, yes," she added, smiling more broadly now. Her teeth were small and perfectly white. "Don't worry, Mr. Fowler,

I'm not carrying any tracts in my pocketbook, I didn't come here to convert you."

"I didn't think that at all, Mrs. Porter."

"Atlanta. You may call me Atlanta."

"Atlanta. I never thought there was any other reason for coming here beside your concern for Stephen."

"No, that's true."

Her smile faded, and she sat silently awhile, staring down in her lap. Something in her expression annoyed me; it seemed both studied and familiar.

Then I realized I'd seen Stephen wear the same suffering, saintly face a few days earlier.

"About the pills," she said, without looking up. "They were mine. Holland doesn't know."

The school where I attended kindergarten was named after President William McKinley, one of the seven presidents who came from Ohio. My mother dropped this choice bit of history in my lap the night before my first day of school, while she was laying out my clothes.

"McKinley is a public school," she explained. "You're only going there because there aren't any Catholic schools that offer kindergarten classes. After kindergarten, you'll go to Mother of Sorrows, which is named after the mother of Jesus."

She paused momentarily to pick several of the more egregious pills from the navy blue cardigan handed down to me from some distant cousin or other on her side of the family.

"The children who go to Catholic school learn manners," she continued, after banishing the little balls of wool to the plastic trash pail beside my bed. "Which are essential for getting ahead in the world. They also learn respect, which is also important. Children who don't learn respect often grow up to be *delinquents*."

Sometimes, when I went grocery shopping with my mother, she'd point out delinquents loitering along the side of Beuckman's grocery store on Route 9. Most were fourteen-to sixteen-year-old boys who wore their collars rolled up and smoked cigarettes. Sideburns that grew down past the ears were another sure sign of delinquency.

My mother was supposed to take me to McKinley on the first day of school, but when morning came, she was too sick to move out of bed. My father had already left for work in a mine up near St. Clairesville, so my grandmother had to dress me hurriedly in my hand-me-down school clothes. Afterward, she combed my hair. Since I was prone to cowlicks, this was a complicated process involving a fair amount of Nestle's hair grooming gel, a thick green ooze dispensed from a plastic bottle with a lady's face on the label.

Unfortunately, my grandmother couldn't take me to school because she had a job. She was a *woman,* cleaning people's houses three days a week. My mother didn't like me to say so in front of other people, however. *It doesn't sound nice,* she told me, quietly but firmly, indicating that no further discussion was allowed.

I ended up walking to school with Toby Hewitt and his mother, who lived two houses up the hill from us. Mrs. Hewitt was small, thin woman with curly brown hair and cat's eye glasses. The rims of her glasses were blue. She tended to walk too fast on stubby high heel shoes, and her mouth was habitually drawn up tight, causing the pale blond hairs around her lips to stand up nearly straight.

Mrs. Hewitt was one of the women who had come by nearly every day to sit with my mother after her miscarriage. One afternoon, I heard shouting from the other side of my mother's bedroom door, after which Mrs. Hewitt hurried from the room, her mouth pinched tighter than ever and her blond whiskers quivering. When she saw me standing in the hall between the kitchen and the bedroom, she smiled a bit too broadly, like the wolf in the fairy tale.

"Nosy Parker should be outside playing in the fresh air," she said, in a tone of voice meant to convey quite a bit more friendly concern than her expression suggested.

Toby Hewitt had dark hair like his mother, but he was big and heavy-set like his father. At five years old, he was already wearing husky-size clothes, and his stomach hung over his pants. Because I'd known him all my life, of course, I didn't think of him as fat. He was just Toby. I didn't think of him as mean, either, although I'd seen him use his father's cigarette lighter to burn spiders alive—their pale brown bodies curling and emitting an abrupt, liquid hiss. I'd also seen him try to shoot birds with his slingshot. He wasn't a very good shot, however, and the stones consistently flew wide of their mark. The best I'd ever seen him do was hit a tree branch, shaking the leaves and sending the birds twittering and squawking across the sky.

On the first day of kindergarten, Toby and I were accompanied by Dana Pulaski and his mother, who lived a little farther up the hill. Mrs. Pulaski was blond and pretty like the women in the magazines my mother fliped through in the supermarket. Dana was blond, like his mother, but even as a child he had a serious, thin face. He had gray eyes and he excelled at physical tasks like running, jumping, swimming, and climbing trees. He was also polite in the way that parents noticed and held up as an example of good behavior.

Mrs. Pulaski walked a few feet behind us, alongside Mrs. Hewitt, gazing down at the sidewalk and nodding while Mrs. Hewitt chattered in a low, sibilant voice almost directly in her ear. Every few minutes I glanced back, trying to figure out what she was saying. I had a pretty good idea it had to do with my mother.

Once, Mrs. Hewitt caught me looking back, and flashed me a quick, lupine smile. "Don't worry precious," she said, her voice sharp and stinging. "We're right behind y'uns."

As we rounded the corner onto Route 9, we met up with another member of the neighborhood clique, Charlie Holubeck, who stood waiting for us with his mother on the sidewalk in front of their house. Mrs. Holubeck was heavy, short woman with slightly exaggerated features that looked like they'd been stuck on her face in a hurry. She joined the other two mothers, waddling slightly in her heavy, white orthopedic shoes.

Charlie fell in beside me. For the first day of school, his mother had dressed him up in a bow tie and a blue cardigan sweater with gold buttons. She also made him carry a small leather portfolio with pencils, paper, crayons, and a ruler in it. The two other mothers made little yips of amusement when they saw him all dressed up like a miniature business man, and commented several times over about how *precious* he looked. Listening to them go on like that made me furious. I spent the rest of the way to school imagining myself dressed up in a bow tie and cardigan instead of hand-me-downs from some cousin of my mother's whom I'd never even met.

William McKinley school was a three-story building built of dark bricks, the color of raw meat. Inside, the walls were painted a pale, soupy green shade—or for variety, a pale, soupy yellow. One side of my classroom was hung with cardboard cutouts of Snow White, Cinderella, and Little Red Riding Hood; about a dozen little girls sat at a long, low table underneath them. Toby, Dana, and I sat at the boys' table on the other side of the room, beneath pictures of Paul Bunyan, Davy Crockett, and an Indian brave.

Some of the mothers were already seated in chairs at the back of the classroom. Mrs. Hewitt and Mrs. Pulaski stood in line with the other mothers who were registering their children with the kindergarten teacher, who sat at her desk nodding and writing names in the register. She seemed older than most of the mothers; her face looked bony and very tan, and her mouth was more or less a thick smear of pink lipstick. She wore a small, flat bow clipped on the side of her honey-colored hair, which was how I was able to remember her name: Mrs. Goodbow.

When Mrs. Hewitt reached the head of the registration line, I watched her point to Toby, smiling as she peered over Mrs. Goodbow's shoulder to make sure she'd spelled the name right. Then her face wrinkled in what appeared to be concern as she ducked her head to whisper something. In response, Mrs. Goodbow looked up from the register and stared across the room at me, one eyebrow raised, the pink smear of a mouth turning downward. She nodded slowly, after which Mrs. Hewitt, smiling primly and clutching her purse in front of her, joined the other mothers at the back of the room. It seemed to me that something sharp and dangerous had passed between them, like a poison dart.

I knew very well that if my mother had come with me, I'd have been spared such peril. In spite of her difficult ways, my mother knew how to charm people. On more than one occasion, I'd watched her coax Oleg—the sour old Russian who ran the package store in Marysville, next town over from Amity—to give her a pound of cold cuts on credit. I'd witnessed her manipulate the Wheeling librarian whenever she was caught pinching magazines from the library. I'd stood next to her in the donut shop, while she wheedled the clerk out of pastries we couldn't afford.

My mother was like water, easily adapting herself to whatever obstacle she encountered. She could make herself just as sour as Oleg, swearing bitterly about the goddamn mining companies that didn't pay a living wage to honest laborers. With the woman who ran the public library in Wheeling—who seemed to be fighting a losing battle with blouse buttons and the bobby pins that held her gray hair in place—she appeared equally harried: apologizing profusely for neglecting to check out the magazines, condemning herself for being so forgetful, juggling purse, coat, and other items as she hurried over to the check-out desk. In the donut store, she'd merely have to shake her head no and smile sadly down at me like the Mother of Jesus, and the price of an eclair would drop from fifty cents to a quarter.

She entered each role with the subtlety and conviction of an artist. No one could accuse her of merely pretending. I never saw her, for example, revert to some sort of normal or neutral self as soon as we stepped outside the library or the donut shop or Oleg's package store.

Still, I did notice a difference between the way she carried herself around other people and the way she behaved when no one was watching. She was never as bright or charming without an audience. At home, she tended to shuffle dully from room to room, complaining of headaches.

There were times, of course, when her mood suddenly lifted—usually when my father and grandmother were away from home. On such occasions, she declared that she felt like a bird released. She'd put Dinah Shore or Patti Page on the hi-fi and, with one hand on my shoulder and clasping my free hand in hers, show me how to dance. I found it a bit difficult to grasp the fundamentals, and early lessons often ended abruptly after I'd stepped on her feet once too often. But after a while the plaintive rhythm of the singer's satiny voice began to trickle into my bones and muscles, and I found myself moving easily in time with the music.

To this day, I remain indebted to my mother for teaching me this fundamental skill.

"You take after my side of the family," she used to say, smiling as we waltzed or fox-trotted around the living room. "We come from a long line of Irish kings and princes, you know. Unlike *other* people."

Those other people were my father and grandmother, who, according to my mother, were descended from a long line of *plebeians.*

"You're going to be good looking when you grow up," she added, studying my face. "But that's not enough to get you out of this hole. You'll have to use your brains. You'll have to be smart."

Unfortunately, being smart didn't make a favorable impression on Mrs. Goodbow. As soon as the mothers had left the classroom on the first day of kindergarten, she called our attention to a long, white strip of paper hanging above the blackboard at the front of the classroom. Each letter of the alphabet had been carefully printed in black ink, along with a picture to help us remember the corresponding sound.

"*A is for apple, B is for boy,*" she chanted, pointing to each letter with a long, thin stick. Afterward, she urged us to chant along with her.

Next, she showed us how to combine the letters to form words, first pointing to the letters with her stick, then writing the combinations on the blackboard. The words were simple: *cat, dog, ant, red, ball.* We parroted them back while Mrs. Goodbow pointed with her stick and spread her greasy pink lips into a smile.

Events took a more challenging turn when she erased the blackboard and invited us to try spelling words on our own.

"Who can spell the word *cat* for me?" she asked, making a show of gazing out over a sea of potential geniuses before settling on a sullen, dark-haired girl named Iris Kimmelbach.

The girl timidly approached the front of the room and took the pointer from Mrs. Goodbow, who looked as though she'd like to swallow her whole in a single bite. Painfully, Iris pondered the symbols just above her head before slowly moving the pointer to spell *C-A-R*.

"I'm sorry Iris, that's not quite right," Mrs. Goodbow said, in a bright voice that suggested that she wasn't sorry at all. She sent Iris back to her seat and gazed out once more over our heads. "Who else would like to try?"

I'd been able to read since I was three years old, thanks to a system my mother had learned from one her purloined copies of the *Reader's Digest.* For several months, she'd taped neatly handwritten signs to common objects around the house. From there, she proceeded to paste together a reader's scrapbook, cutting pictures out of magazines and printing words underneath. By the age of five, I could breeze through *The Gingerbread Man* or *The Little Engine That Could* several times in one sitting, a feat that never failed to elicit praise and a piece of Hershey's chocolate from old Mrs. Hodge, who lived next door to my grandmother.

Now, motivated as much by impatience as by a desire to set myself in Mrs. Goodbow's good graces, I blurted out, "C-A-T!"

Instead of being impressed, however, Mrs. Goodbow gave me a sour look.

"When we have something to say, we raise our hands," she said stiffly. "And we speak when we're called on. Is that clear?"

All eyes turned toward me as, speechless, I merely nodded in reply. For the first time I could remember, I began to sweat for reasons that had nothing to do with hot weather or physical exertion.

"We can't have everybody gibbering like monkeys in a zoo, now can we?" Mrs. Goodbow continued, smiling broadly and inviting the rest of the class to laugh at the comparison. Even the obviously moronic Iris Kimmelbach snickered—relieved, I think, that her own humiliation had been smoothed over so adroitly.

From then on, though I raised my hand diligently and often, Mrs. Goodbow refused to call on me. By the end of my first week in kindergarten, I made up my mind that I wouldn't answer anything unless she addressed me directly.

September passed without further incident, and around Halloween we were busily engaged in making witches out of black construction paper. At the front of the classroom, Mrs. Goodbow demonstrated a complicated technique of cutting, folding, and gluing the paper to make two cones: a larger one for the witch's body and a smaller one for her pointed hat. The smaller cone was to be glued onto a construction paper circle that formed the brim of the hat. The main thing, she told us, was to work carefully and slowly, saving our scraps to make the witch's arms, feet, and broom.

I approached the task with intense concentration, artfully shaping a perfect cone for the witch's body and an equally impressive one for her hat. Unfortunately, when I glanced up from my work, I discovered most of the rest of the class had already finished their work and sat in front of neatly cleared places. I hastily clamped my witch's hat on her body and cleaned up my work area.

A few minutes later, Mrs. Goodbow proceeded down the aisle between our tables, examining our efforts. She stopped just behind my chair.

"Where are her arms, Christian?" she asked. "Where's her broom?"

In my hurry to finish I'd forgotten to attach my witch's appendages. Worse still, I'd already cleaned up my area and thrown away my scraps.

"She doesn't need them," I replied. She was a witch, after all, I reasoned; if she had magic, what did she need arms for?

Unfortunately, Mrs. Goodbow didn't see things in quite the same way, and while everyone else was released to the free play area at the back of the classroom, I had to remain at the table cutting out scraps from a fresh piece of construction paper.

The sense of such activity eluded me. A person didn't set out to make scraps; scraps were left over from something else. Even more upsetting was the humiliation of being excluded from free play in full view of my classmates. Childish indignation gathered inside my chest as I attacked the construction paper with my scissors.

Then a curious thing happened.

A piece of my mind seemed to separate itself from the rest, and I actually watched myself choose to march up to Mrs. Goodbow's desk and slam the scraps down in front of her.

"Here are your *scraps*!" I announced in a loud voice.

I recognized my voice, my hand. I also recognized beyond doubt that nothing good would come of what I'd just done. And yet the part of me that made these evaluations remained oddly peaceful, as though looking down from a great distance.

Mrs. Goodbow didn't respond immediately. Then, abruptly, her mouth opened like a dead fish's, and she reached across her desk so fast I hardly saw her move. Her fingers clamped down hard on my arm.

"Don't you ever use that tone of voice in my classroom again," she said slowly, pausing between every word.

All of a sudden I was crying—gulping, wracking sobs that shook my whole body. Without letting go of my arm, Mrs. Goodbow stood and pivoted around her desk and half-dragged me out of the classroom into the hallway, closing the door behind us with her free hand. She used the pressure on my arm to force me to sit down with my back against the wall. Then she stood there with her arms folded across her chest, watching me cry.

A moment later, a bald, stoop-shouldered man with tufts of white hair erupting from his ears came toward us: the McKinley School principal.

"What's the matter here?" he asked.

"We're just a little overwrought," Mrs. Goodbow lied. "I thought it would be better if we came out here to calm down."

The principal nodded and continued down the hall. As soon as he had moved out of earshot, Mrs. Goodbow turned back to me, narrowing her eyes.

"Crybaby," she hissed.

Normally, I'd walk home from school with Toby Hewitt and Dana Pulaski. The route was simple and direct: a left turn down Route 9 and then another left up the hill. Since we went to morning kindergarten, it was always broad daylight when we were released and there was hardly any traffic. On the day of my public humiliation, however, I couldn't wait for Toby and Dana, but charged up the road on my own. All I wanted was to get home and shut the door behind me. As far as I was concerned, going back to Mrs. Goodbow's room again was completely out of the question.

My grandmother's house was utterly quiet when I returned, and no one answered when I called hello. I tiptoed through the kitchen, after concluding that my mother was either sleeping or suffering from one of her bad headaches.

I realized I was wrong as soon as I reached the threshold between the kitchen and the dark hall leading down to my parents' bedroom. Even in the dim light I could see my mother stretched out in front of the bathroom. She was just lying there naked and still, face down.

For the second time that day, I felt a piece of myself break away and float up to a place where I could simply watch my body and hear my voice without any particular investment in the outcome. I could even feel my heart churning in my chest, but it didn't worry me. I headed up the street calculating that although old Mrs. Hodge would be more sympathetic about the situation, she couldn't move very quickly. The next best option was to ring the Hewitt's doorbell.

Mrs. Hewitt came to the door wearing an apron over her dress. Pink plastic curlers peeked over the sash of toilet paper wrapped around her hair.

Calmly, I informed her that my mother was dead.

"*Wha—?*" she gasped, unable even to complete the question.

Then she pushed the screen door open, grabbed my hand, and took off running toward our house. She hadn't even taken the time to put her shoes on, and the backs of her loose slippers made slapping sounds on the sidewalk. Inside, she fumbled for the light switch and hurried down the hall, slowing only as she reached my mother's body and knelt down over it.

Abruptly, she turned away with a grimace, then turned back and lifted my mother's head. In the light now, I could see that her face was covered with vomit.

"Oh honey, she's not dead," Mrs. Hewitt called out weakly. "She's just—" she searched for the word—"*ill.*"

She continued kneeling there for almost a full minute, clearly not relishing the idea of having to clean up the mess. Then she stood and entered my mother's room, emerging moments later with a bed sheet. She draped the sheet around my mother to conceal her nakedness as she dragged her by the arms back into the bedroom. I could hear sounds of puffing and straining from inside the room, but Mrs. Hewitt didn't respond to my offer of help.

After a while, she came back out into the hall, curlers and toilet paper askew, her mouth a grim line. She stepped into the bathroom, wet a washcloth, and headed back into the bedroom. Moments later, she emerged once again and stooped to wipe up the congealed puddle of vomit on the floor. When she'd finished, she wrote a quick note to my father and grandmother and dropped it on the kitchen table. Then she took me by the hand back up the hill to her house.

Inside, she called for Toby. He wasn't home, which was just as well. Mrs. Hewitt sat me at the kitchen table and methodically proceeded to make a sandwich of peanut butter and butter, which she served on a plate painted with a border of small purple flowers. Then she left the room and I heard her walk across the hall into the living room and call Mrs. Pulaski.

"Ida," she murmured, "it's Helen Hewitt, is Toby there? I thought so."

It took hardly any effort for my ears to adjust to the level of her voice.

"No, I actually wasn't here," she continued. "You'll never believe. Chris Fowler showed up on my doorstep, white as a sheet, and said Eileen was dead. So naturally I raced down there . . . No, she wasn't. Dead *drunk* is more like it."

The detached part of my mind could almost see her on the telephone, smiling smugly, the blond whiskers around her lips twitching like the legs of some poisonous insect. Slowly, I laid my sandwich back down on the plate, arranging it so that it sat perfectly centered inside the border of purple flowers.

"No, he's here, poor thing," she went on, maliciously. "Yes, I fixed him some lunch. Well, I know, in a house like that, God knows when the last time was he even had something proper to eat."

Stealthily, on cat feet, I stood up from the table and sidled out the kitchen door.

Though I'm a reasonably good driver, every once in a while I'm overwhelmed by the idea that I'm piloting a machine capable of inflicting tremendous damage. One of the reasons I enjoy living in a city full of transportation options is that I prefer to pass the responsibility for driving onto someone else. I like the security of renting for the same reason. When something goes wrong in the apartment, it's someone else's job to come up and fix it.

That's the theory at least, which really only applies to cosmetic problems: the radiator that spits hot water on the wood floor, the soap dish that suddenly tumbles out of the wall when the shower's running, the windows that rattle every time a taxi rumbles down the street.

Imperfect as it is, I've shared my apartment with Richard for almost ten years. Richard and I are exact opposites in many respects. He is short, wiry, and dark; I am tall, not especially wiry, and fair. Richard is enormously charming, an excellent quality for a doctor. He remembers details about people, about their plans, their vacations, their parents' health; whereas I often find myself stumbling over names.

Richard also tends to see things far more concretely than I do, which may or may not be a by-product of his profession. As a medical doctor, he calculates survival in terms of numbers, percentages, and discrete periods of time. Treatment either produces the desired effect or it fails; his patients live or they die. He feels bad when they die, of course, but he doesn't take it personally.

We even approach our differences differently. I tend to hide emotional discomfort behind a veil of observation. I'm conspicuously reasonable in my acceptance of things as they are.

Richard has affairs.

He's been having one for several months now, in fact, though I'm not sure whether this adds or detracts from his appeal. At the moment, I'm inclined to think it makes him more attractive. If nothing I feel about him is simple, he's harder to deny.

For the last couple of years before my father died, my mother had suspected him of "stepping out." He had begun spending more and more time away from home—usually just driving around the hills in his pickup truck, or fishing, or simply motoring back and forth across the local lake. After he returned, I'd catch my mother examining his shirts for lipstick stains or the scent of strange perfume, or digging around the inside of his truck for earrings.

One evening, she pulled a balled up pair of boxers out of her pocket while we were having dinner.

"What's this?" she demanded.

My father, pausing in mid-chew, told her they looked like underwear.

"There's blood on them," she said. "Right here on the front. How did you get blood on the front of your undershorts?"

My grandmother and I both stopped eating, while my father continued chewing, silently and deliberately. I could see his jaw muscles working hard.

"Is it Ida Pulaski?" my mother asked. "Is she having her period? The two of you just couldn't wait, is that it? Or do you like the feeling of blood on your tit?"

A vein in my father's neck pulsed, and the knuckles of his hand went white as he gripped his fork. He muttered something and then started shaking. With laughter, as it turned out.

"Jesus Christ, Eileen," he said, looking up from his plate. "I got it caught in my zipper."

Seconds later, my grandmother caught his meaning and covered her mouth with the back of her hand. Then her shoulders started to shake, and after exchanging glances with my father, she gave up trying to stop herself from laughing. I joined in, too, then; not because I knew what the joke was—I had yet to undergo that experience—but simply because they were laughing. I didn't want to be left out of it, like my mother, sitting at the kitchen table with a pair of dirty undershorts in her hand.

Evidence of Richard's infidelity is more elusive. Periods throughout the day when he's unreachable, either at his office or the hospital. Too many late nights when he arrives home smiling, not exhausted, smelling freshly showered. Once, it was a Christmas party with people from the hospital he's affiliated with—the first and last such public event we attended together. From a corner where I stood trapped listening to long-winded stories about radiology, I watched him sidle close to a blond, curly-haired number with more teeth than nature deemed necessary. He slid his hand along the young man's back and the two of them exchanged a discreet grin.

Usually, after the initial rage of discovering a new affair wears off, I'll brood about his habit of sleeping with men less than half his age. I find myself actually envying his ability to forget the cracks and scars on his own body, the crude implications of time and gravity. I imagine him sneaking through a door to an enchanted garden, where he can be young again and still know everything he knows;

and I end up forgiving him because I understand the impulse to sneak through a door like that.

I don't go to parties with him anymore, however.

The long drive from Columbus to Amity gives me time to ponder why I continue in a relationship that has become, in many ways, humiliating. I've memorized a few good reasons, which I recite from time to time like a catechism. I tell myself, for example, that infidelity isn't really intolerable. That there are enough strikes against two men trying to live together. That I need to buck my own tendency to leave when I'm uncomfortable.

About a hundred miles outside of Columbus, just as the snow begins to clear, I start to wonder who I think I'm fooling. I care about Richard, of course. In my own way, I believe I love him.

I'm also terribly afraid of being old and alone, like the last of the dinosaurs.

After two hours on the interstate, I can see the land on either side of the highway has begun to change. Hills rise out of darkness, sinewy and muscled like the back of a giant snake. There are more trees here, needled kinds like spruce and hemlock, their branches tipped with snow.

At the exit for Route 9, I turn off the interstate and head southeast into Putnam County, a much darker region where square yellow lights shine intermittently through trees. I pass a snowman tilting at a crazy angle in front of one house; in front of another, the rusty shell of a truck and a bicycle half-buried in the snow. There are no signs to say I've passed from Holyoke to Marysville, from Marysville to Midway, and from Midway to Amity. The formal entrance to my hometown is nothing more than an intersection. On the north side is a concrete shell of a building; on the south, a bar called Haemon's. Between them runs the road that leads up to my grandmother's house.

Hers is the third house up the hill. After stopping the car, all I can do for a while is simply sit staring at the yellow paint bubbling in wide strips along the front. The house seems to shrink away from me, squat, reproachful, and sulking. Probably just a trick of the moon, shining now through patchy clouds. The sky seems thick with stars. One pale light gleams like a clouded eye from a house farther up the hill; otherwise the street is dark.

The barn that once stood at the top of the hill is gone. During the winter of 1965 the old farmer who owned it had walked into Haemon's bar, where his wife used to escape for a drink almost every night, and took off part of her head with a twelve-gauge shotgun. Then he turned the shotgun on himself and spattered his guts across the jukebox. His stock was sold off a few months later, but his sons held onto the property. The barn had stared down from the hill like a ruined face, a place where neighborhood kids went to drink, play cards, and grope each other in the empty stalls.

I didn't go there often. The place was considered something of a proving ground, where young boys tried to outperform each other in feats of seeming masculinity. Each time I went, I felt as though I'd come up lacking.

The barn caught fire the same night I left Amity to go live with my Uncle Ames and Aunt Jane. I didn't stay around to watch it go—I heard from my grandmother later on that the fire had attracted quite a crowd. I wasn't sorry afterward to hear that it had burned to the ground. Certain places become irredeemably linked to the experiences and emotions of childhood. For me, fear will always smell like old hay and rotting wood.

A gust of wind buffets the rental car, cutting short my nostalgic indulgence. After pulling my coat and scarf tight, I step out of the car, grab my suitcase from the backseat, and make my way across the yard. The snow here is smooth and slick, making the passage treacherous.

On the front porch, I kick through the heavy layer of snow until my boot strikes a rock. There's a key frozen solid in the ice beneath, and after trying for a few minutes to dig it out by hand, my fingers feel peeled and bloated. Only then does it occur to me to use my car keys to dig it out.

Of the two entrances on the porch, the one to the parlor is blocked by a fairly impressive snow drift. The one piled against the kitchen door, however, is much smaller, and takes only a few minutes to dislodge—though the wind sends some of the loose snow swirling back into my face. The key, of course, refuses to turn in the lock. I don't know why I should be surprised by the notion of coming this far through a snowstorm only to be defeated by a piece of metal.

Somewhere up the hill, a dog starts howling, which offers little consolation. Then something snaps behind me—a tall horse chestnut across the street, creaking in the wind. I try the key again, more gently, and this time it turns in the lock and the door pops open.

Inside, I feel my way to a light switch, moving slowly, cautiously, as the kitchen comes awake with the sound of mice scrambling to hide. Then the smell hits me: a combination of mildew, ammonia, and something undefinable, like yeast. For a while, all I can do is stand in the middle of the room, breathing in this amalgam of familiar and unfamiliar odors. Gingerly, I lay my hand on the back of a chair, half-expecting it to dissolve under my touch or emit some type of punitive electric charge. But nothing unusual happens; the chair behaves exactly like a chair.

I hang my coat on the back of a chair and step through the arch that leads from the kitchen to what my grandmother used to call the parlor; an old-fashioned word, reminiscent of courtship, fans, young ladies bending over needlepoint. The front door has been boarded shut, and only a narrow window gives light from the street. A sofa, two armchairs, a television set, and a Magnavox hi-fi crowd the small room.

Of the dozen or so framed pictures on the walls, I recognize several of myself as a boy, smiling in front of lopsided Christmas trees and chocolate birthday cakes. Seeing them feels a bit like stumbling upon corpses under ice; the surprise makes me shudder. There's also a hazy, early color photograph of my grandfather dressed in hunting gear, holding up the slit neck of a nine-point buck. And several of my father at various ages: a boy, a young man, and a grinning bridegroom standing beside my mother, a pale, red-haired girl with a giddy smile.

The wedding picture stirs a memory of Stephen, who, after our first meeting, had taken to sitting in my office without saying a word. He'd show up, wait his forty-five minutes, then get up and leave. Naturally, I tried a number of strategies to draw him out: asking questions, mentioning odd things I'd seen or heard, tossing out feelers about sports, politics, school, religion. I tried looking at him, not looking at him. I even tried to match him silence for silence.

After a few weeks, I decided to try a somewhat less orthodox approach.

It was just before Memorial Day. The air in the city had already begun to thicken, and the sidewalks churned with people blinking myopically like bears coming out of hibernation. Bits of conversation—trailing above the noise of taxi horns, the wail of a passing ambulance, the diesel farts of city buses—predicted a long, hot summer. It's possible the heat had made me a little testy.

"How old were you when you moved to New York?" I asked

Stephen, a few minutes into yet another silent session. "Do you remember if it was hard for you to leave? Were there any special friends you didn't want to leave behind? Any family members?"

He sat, not precisely immobile, with his arms folded across his chest, his legs slightly apart. His white-blond eyelashes fluttered a couple of times.

"Because," I continued, "I thought we might talk a little about how people go about missing each other." I waited a few more minutes and then cleared my throat. "My parents, for instance. They grew up in the same town, but they might as well have been strangers. They met on a hayride, actually, which my mother only agreed to go on because her best friend had a boyfriend who had a friend who needed a date. And so on. An old story."

I settled back in my chair—a faded yellow recliner—as Stephen flicked a glance in my direction.

"My mother's date got drunk and passed out in the rick," I went on, "so my father, who was actually my mother's best friend's date for the evening, offered her a ride home. He found her, I think, sweet.

"He drove past her house every day for a month after that, hoping he'd see her again so he could ask her for a proper date. Finally, he saw her one afternoon, rocking back and forth on the porch swing. But he was too afraid to go up to her, and all he could manage to do was slow down his truck and beep the horn as he drove by. This went on for another month, until finally he worked up the courage to get out of his truck and walk up to the porch and introduce himself. My mother replied that she remembered him well enough, and that in fact she'd been waiting on the porch every day hoping he'd drive by. Their timing had been off, was all. She was just your age, Stephen. Sixteen."

The coincidence, alas, failed to draw him in.

"My mother's family didn't like my father—a coal miner living in a shabby little house in a shabby little town—and since he was not a particularly assertive sort of person, it fell to my mother to come up with a plan. She convinced him to take her out for a ride at night in the little motorboat he'd bought secondhand with part of his first year's wages from the mines. If she could've arranged the rain she'd have probably done it, but that came down of its own accord. My mother told my father not to turn the boat around and so they huddled for a long while together in the dark and the damp. Which was, actually, how I was conceived. In a rocking boat in the middle of a rainstorm."

I stopped talking suddenly, staring down at my hands like someone who's forgotten the punch line to a long and ultimately not terribly funny joke.

After a minute, Stephen shifted on the couch, gingerly adjusting his legs as though they'd fallen asleep.

"What am I supposed to do?" he said quietly—the first words he'd spoken in six weeks. "Am I supposed to feel sorry for you? Boo hoo, I'm crying."

I didn't look up, afraid he'd retreat if I did.

"I just thought we might talk," I replied. "Exchange stories. Maybe we could come to understand each other a little better."

"I understand you good enough."

The spiteful, adolescent certainty in his tone struck my ears with an aching familiarity. It reminded me, not of my own past self—if anything, I'd always tended to hide behind a habit of nearly pathological courtesy toward my elders—but of a boy named Reis Paley, whom I'd known very briefly during my last year in Amity. He had the same sort of verbal swagger, the same air of self-sufficiency. It's possible I'd even heard the same phrase from him a long time ago; or at least something fairly similar.

Abruptly, time as I understood it rolled over on itself, and for a long, disorienting moment I was sure Stephen knew things that would have been impossible for him to know.

My own silence seemed to surprise him.

"So," he asked, "what happened?"

"Oh well," I replied, "things turned out more or less the way you'd expect." I risked a glance at him now. He'd sunk farther down, and though he kept his arms folded across his thin chest, he'd allowed the back of his head to rest against the top of the couch. "One of my mom's brothers showed up looking for my father. Unfortunately for him, my grandmother came to the door with one of my grandfather's deer hunting rifles and chased him down the street. I heard it was quite a spectacle, this big Irishman running away from a little old lady screeching in Polish.

"At any rate, my parents got married a couple of months later. My mother fainted in the middle of the ceremony because her dress was too tight. They spent their wedding night in Wheeling, which was pretty much all the honeymoon they could afford."

"So you ain't rich then?" Stephen asked.

"No. It would be nice, but no."

"How come you act like you are?"

"What do you mean?"

"You act snooty. Smiling like your shit don't stink."

"Really?" I replied, not precisely displeased, but surprised. "I had no idea."

He smiled then—the first real look of pleasure I'd seen from him—and spread his arms across the back of the couch.

"What else have you noticed?" I asked.

His smile broadened and he shook his head slowly back and forth. "You're all the same, ain't you?"

When I asked what he meant, he only blew through his lips and sank farther back in the couch. I pressed him, trying to keep the tone light, asking who were all the same? Therapists? Adults? Men with blond hair?

"Faggots," he replied.

We sat for a while, listening to the soft hum from the air conditioner across the alley from my office.

"Why do you think I'm a faggot?" I asked.

He sneered, which was more than I'd expected. I picked up a pencil from the table beside my chair and balanced it between two fingers.

"I mean," I continued after a minute, "I assume you have your reasons."

Abruptly, Stephen flushed and the veins in his neck bulged.

"Don't tell me any of that takes one to know one," he replied. "I heard that one before and it's bull."

Everything in the room suddenly appeared small and distant, as though seen through the wrong end of a telescope. I could only compare the experience to the shift in perspective that sometimes accompanies a high fever; and when the moment had passed, I felt nearly the same wrung-out feeling.

"Stephen," I replied, as gently as possible, "I hardly know you. How can I have any special understanding about you?"

His hands, clutching the sofa cushions, spasmed. Still, he managed to shrug. "People say such things."

"Yes, they do."

We sat. Gradually, the color faded from Stephen's skin, his breathing became more normal.

"We can make a pact," I said. "How about if I only believe the things you tell me."

"And what?"

"And you say whatever you want. Be *people*. Say *things*. I don't really give a damn what you say, but I am interested in the way you think about things."

He sat several seconds longer pressing himself as far back into the couch cushions as possible. Then he looked down at his hands, surprised, it seemed, to see them still clenching and unclenching. He willed them to stop, then slowly relaxed his body until he was resting in his usual position against the arm of the sofa.

I thought maybe I'd won a round, at last. That I'd broken through some barrier or defense. But the longer he sat, the more clear it became that I hadn't won anything at all.

He'd simply retreated.

At the end of the session, he stood up without a word and left the office.

I beat a hasty retreat now back into my grandmother's kitchen. The walls here are covered with the same floral paper I remember from twenty years ago. Water stains have blurred the color in several places, melting the blossoms into strange, ungainly shapes. If I look too closely, they might turn out to be faces, so I turn my attention elsewhere—to the disorder, which feels wrong.

My grandmother had always been fastidious. But now that I'm ready to take in details, I can see several drawers hanging open and a stack of dirty dishes in the sink. There's even a splotch of jelly on the tablecloth. The general untidiness reminds me of stories I've heard from patients whose elderly parents have grown forgetful, or even vindictively chaotic. For an instant, I envision my grandmother in a filthy housecoat, with greasy hair in tangles like Medusa, muttering to herself as she shuffles barefoot through the house, banging doors open and tossing things on the floor.

I can't connect this ghost, however, with my grandmother—who managed, after all, to write once a month right up until the end. Her letters were full of homely details about her flower garden, or the vegetables she managed to can in the fall, or the activities of the young couple who moved in next door after Mrs. Hodge finally died. She never bothered to write about the people I used to know. She never rambled.

I can only imagine that she must have simply felt out of sorts, and decided to leave the kitchen till morning.

Beyond the kitchen is a narrow hall lined with cheap paneling, scratched and dented in many places, and I can probably put a date on each scar I made as a boy. Cobwebs sway from the ceiling like tiny trapeze ropes.

A flight of stairs at the end of the hall leads to the attic, which my father had converted into a bedroom for me when I was four years old. The stairs lead straight into my room; there's no door, no landing where I can rest a minute and gather courage. I flick on the light at the top of the stairs and there's my old bed, just as I remember it, in the far corner, under the window. Even the bedspread is the same, maroon with yellow and blue stripes, which I actually don't remember until I see it again, and then all its associations surge back: anxious nights listening to my parents fighting downstairs, nights of planning what I'd do to get back at my father or mother or grandmother for what seemed draconian punishments, anxious nights before the start of a new school year, seemingly endless nights before Christmas.

Next to my bed, a bookcase tilts at the same angle as the floor. At the other end of room stands a dresser with eagle emblems pasted on the drawers, a relic of my mother's abortive attempt to impose a unifying Colonial motif on the odd assortment of furniture in the house.

It would be easy to give in to nostalgia at a moment like this, except that the disorder seems more deliberate up here than it did down in the kitchen. My dresser drawers have all been emptied out, and my old clothes scattered on the floor. My old books have been pulled from the shelves. I pick one up as I cross the room, and a sheaf of yellowed papers falls out. I hardly recognize the boyish penmanship, the precise squares and circles, yet it's my name written on the top line.

Something beyond the mess itself disturbs me.

A pattern—or more precisely, a lack thereof—that doesn't fit the way a habitually neat person would look for things, even in a hurry.

It takes an effort of will to begin the process of straightening up, folding clothes and putting them back in drawers, returning the books to their shelves, nudging furniture back into place. I'm sure there must be a message in the chaos, some sort of accidental signal of intent. But it's late, my knees throb on the bare wood floor, and it's so cold in the house that I can almost see my breath.

It's only when I give up trying to tease out the unconscious message and turn to something prosaic like stripping the bed that I finally find the sign I was looking for: an oily sort of stain on the quilt shaped like a man's boot.

I assume it's a man's, at any rate; it's far too big to be my grandmother's.

Reason tells me that any intruder surprised by my unexpected arrival has had ample time to slip away while I've been banging around the house. Unfortunately, the fear I find myself choking back as I head downstairs is anything but reasonable. It's not provoked by thoughts of a flesh-and-blood burglar. What causes my heart to beat is pure childhood fancy. Nameless, faceless creatures that can materialize out of walls or shadows. Monstrous things that devour little boys and grown men impartially.

Standing outside my parents' bedroom, I almost hear an echo of the voices that used to break the stillness of winter nights. *Why can't I touch you, you're my wife.* My mother's moans crawling up through the floorboards of my bedroom. In the mornings she might have a puffy lip, or he'd have a scratch along his temple, near the eye. During the day, she'd lie in bed drinking and nursing dreams, while my father dug coal or took his boat out on the lake.

What I actually hear is a soft scratching sound on the other side of the door. Which could be mice. I take a breath and throw open the door, snapping my hand around the frame to flick on the light. The bulb is burned out, naturally.

Still, enough light shines in from the hall to let me see the window shade flapping against the sash; which makes the scratching sound I'd heard earlier. As I cross the room, my boots crunch on broken glass. Now I can see a hole in the window, just big enough for a hand to come through.

I'm more angry than afraid, as though someone had dug up my grandmother's grave, or even harmed her physically. The feeling of violation is almost nauseating. I stuff a pillow in the broken pane, then go to the kitchen to look for the broom, which is hanging where it has always hung, on a hook behind the cellar door.

In my hurry to sweep up, I manage to cut my finger. Not deeply, but enough to soil three Band-Aids before the bleeding finally stops. By the time I'm through, I've managed to drip blood on the bathroom sink and on the floor. I've even gotten some on my shirt, so I strip it off and leave it soaking in the sink. Far more nimbly than I'd imagined possible, I sprint back upstairs to put on a new shirt and a sweater, then head back down to find the thermostat and turn up the heat.

Seeking other signs of intrusion, I move through the other rooms in the house too quickly, like an angry ghost. The sense of slow, almost tranquil, decay contrasts sharply with the life I'm used to in New York, which typically feels like a pitched battle between gravity and inertia. I should probably watch my step. If I'm not careful, I could be seduced by the steady rhythm of disintegration.

Though it's after midnight, I decide to call New York. I feel the need to cut myself on the few stakes I've left planted in the world of the living.

"It's me," I announce, when Richard answers the phone.

I hear covers rustling on the bed—our bed—and wonder who else is there with him. Someone blond, nineteen or twenty, pulling the sheets around himself now in an unconscious gesture to protect himself against me, the dragon on the other end of the phone line. I feel like Medea.

"You made it," Richard says. "I was getting worried. What's it like?"

"The house is in fairly bad shape," I reply. "Cold. I hope the furnace hasn't burned out, or whatever it is furnaces do."

"Can't you go to a hotel?"

This makes me laugh. "I think Joseph and Mary would've had an easier time finding a place to stay."

"They can't all be booked."

"There aren't any hotels, Richard. This is rural America at its most rural."

"Oh."

"I passed a couple of motels, actually, but they're not the kind you'd feel safe taking a shower in."

Silence, cold and crystalline as the snow outside, settles over the telephone line.

"You still there?" Richard asks. "I can't hear you suddenly."

"I'm sorry. The connection's bad. Or the phone maybe. It's probably an antique."

"Bring it home then."

"What?"

"I said bring it home."

"Oh. Yes."

I'm starting to feel foolish. Richard's probably figured out by now that I only called because I didn't expect to find him home. We've outgrown the part where we worry if we don't hear from each other after eleven at night. Not that bad things don't happen, of course. It's just that we tend to go to bed earlier now.

"You must be tired," he says.

"I suppose. Probably. Yes."

"I miss you."

I don't know what surprises me more: that he's said it, or the earnest tone that makes me want to believe him.

"Me, too," I reply.

As I hang up the phone, I realize I mean it.

I feel suddenly exhausted.

It's a little tricky changing the bed with only one hand, but I don't want to take the chance of getting blood on the clean sheets, which feel cold and stiff as I slip between them. I can't tell if the furnace is actually making a difference or not. Even so, in a matter of minutes I can feel myself spinning down a dark tunnel, into dreams full of snow, and sirens, and other strange noises.

I wake up once, just before dawn. Milky light filters through the window behind my bed and the room is so cold that my ears and the tip of my nose hurt. At first, I can't place the sound that woke me: the steady drip of water into a basin. Then I remember leaving my shirt in the bathroom sink.

I consider getting out of bed and going downstairs to tighten the tap or drain the sink, but I can't make myself face the cold. Instead, I pull the covers up to my chin and wrap the pillow around my ears to block the sound.

The image of something floating in water nags at me for a long time. I think about the broken window and the mess.

Though logic does not connect these things, I know they are connected.

Even so, it's fairly cold comfort to realize that the person I'm looking for may also be looking for me.

Hunting

My father was a hunter, and on my tenth birthday he decided I was old enough to join him in the sport. Accordingly, every weekend throughout the summer and fall, we drove out to the Putnam County dump. After parking the truck outside the fence, we moved to an isolated area of the dump, where he set up cans and bottles for me to practice on.

"This's the way my pap taught me," he said, the first time he set up the targets.

The remark surprised me. When he spoke at all, my father usually limited his observations to immediate circumstances, such as the current weather or the meal on his plate. From the occasional throbbing of the vein in his forehead and his habit of mouthing words quietly to himself, I inferred that his outward stillness didn't necessarily reflect an inner equanimity. Given my mother's penchant for using words vindictively, I believed he'd chosen silence as a less harmful alternative.

So this uncharacteristic personal revelation, though trivial, weighed significantly in my mind. I imagined a long line of Fowler fathers teaching their sons the skills that would fit them for survival in the harsh world. I began to feel something quite strong toward my father. I'm not sure I would have called it love; it felt much more like acute discomfort.

Whatever it was seemed to make my father uncomfortable, too. After that first lesson I don't remember him often giving me a hug or a pat on the back, or even rubbing his hand in my hair. Without explanation or warning, any expression of affection between us was tacitly forbidden.

Over the next several months, my father taught me to square my feet and tuck the rifle butt against the fleshy part of my upper chest just below my shoulder, so the recoil wouldn't break my collar bone. He also showed me how to gauge the accuracy of a gun's sights, and compensate for variation. My hopes of becoming an expert marksman—or at least of demonstrating some sort of innate and workable genius—were quickly revised by actual experience, however. It came as something of a shock to me that a sport with such a bluntly violent end required such complex and delicate precision. Eventually, I developed some skill and reliability. Though by no means the worst marksman Ohio had ever produced, I knew I was a far cry from the best.

My father kept whatever hopes and disappointments he'd formed regarding my progress in strict reserve. Though I have no doubt his silence on this point was motivated by kindness, the lack of response was less than encouraging.

When October arrived, and I was able to consistently demolish six out of every ten targets, I gathered my courage and asked him what he thought of my shooting.

He stood still for so long, just staring at the ground and nodding, that I thought he hadn't heard me. At the last second, he raised his head and formed his mouth into what seemed a pained, if genuine, smile.

"It's good as can be, you know," he replied.

Then, perhaps realizing his answer lacked the degree of enthusiasm a ten-year-old boy might require at such a moment, he added, "It's good."

In early December, he announced that I was ready for my first hunt. We left the house before sunrise, and though there wasn't much snow, the air was bitterly cold. I had to wear long johns beneath my clothes, and a wool hat and hunting jacket that had been my father's when he was my age. I felt both apprehensive and excited by the prospect of putting the months of practice into actual service.

The one discordant element was the inclusion of Toby Hewitt, whose father had recently been confined to bed with the miner's curse, emphysema.

By age ten, Toby had metamorphosed from a merely husky boy into a frankly heavy one. Ashamed of his big gut and heavy breasts, he routinely wore a T-shirt whenever he went swimming in the creek or the Putnam County public pool. His black, curly hair was usually matted and flaked with dandruff, and he smelled like stale sweat.

His eyes had a sly, slitted look—due in part to the fatty folds of flesh around the lids, and in part to genuine guile. He had a way of suggesting things so that you'd feel stupid if you disagreed with him. His particular modus operandi was to insinuate that other boys we knew were too cowardly to do the things he wanted to do.

"Andy Kreuer doesn't have the nuts to snitch a beer from crazy Oleg," he'd say. Or, "Ray Wellhauser's too much of a sissy to ask his mom for a stupid extra dollar just to take a friend to the movies."

I didn't entirely believe these accusations, but I didn't want him to refer to me in the same way. I usually did what he asked, no matter how uncomfortable it made me.

Which was how he came to tag along on my first hunting trip.

We'd been watching television in his basement, keeping the sound low so it wouldn't disturb his father, who was resting in a bedroom two stories above us. Almost as soon as I'd mentioned the trip, I regretted saying anything at all. From the stiff way that Toby sat, I could tell he was trying to figure out a way to invite himself along without seeming to.

At last, after about five minutes, he sighed and I steeled myself for the worst.

"I wish my dad wasn't sick," he mumbled. "You're so lucky."

I was so surprised by this uncharacteristic display of honesty that I told him I'd ask my father if he could come along, too. Toby turned to me with a bright, loopy, and utterly sincere-seeming grin.

"You will? Really?" he asked.

When I replied affirmatively, he dropped one heavy, smelly arm on my shoulder and told me what a pal I was.

"Not like Charlie Holubeck," he added. "You have to practically twist his leg off to get him to ask his dad for a goddamn thing."

The early morning dark imposed its stillness on us all as we headed toward the hunting site. After half an hour on the road, my father pulled to a stop on the shoulder of the Route 9 and he, Toby, and I rolled out of the truck and gulped down the frozen air.

My father unloaded the guns from the back of the truck. He handed one to Toby and one to me before we started climbing through the woods on our right. The rocks and stones poking through the ground looked like the tops of skulls; the tree roots covered in webs of frost looked like bones.

My father pointed out a stand behind a clump of trees. Toby sat down awkwardly, tired and red-faced from the climb. Every so often my father looked over and grinned encouragingly at us, the breath leaking white from the corners of his mouth. I grinned back with steadily diminishing enthusiasm as my arms and legs grew stiff from the cold and the waiting.

Slowly, the sky faded to silver, then pink, and at last to a fine, rose-veined pearl. By then we'd been waiting so long I thought I was only imagining the thickening in the shadows on the other side of the clearing. But the longer I stared, the more certain I became, until softly, like a secret manifestation of the forest's heart, out of the trees stepped a deer.

None of us moved for a moment. The buck stood serene, the morning sun playing along its body. Almost daintily, it turned to nose the bark of a tree and then stopped, flicking its head to stare across the clearing. I wondered if it had seen or heard us, sensed our presence somehow. I hoped it had. I hoped it would run.

The blast from my rifle knocked me flat. I blacked out for a few seconds, until the sound of screaming pulled me back, and from a weird, sprawled perspective I watched my father pushing through the trees and Toby plunging through after him, still screaming. My head and shoulder throbbed as I shuffled to a standing position. Up ahead somewhere, Toby had stopped screaming, but the trail of blood through the trees was clear enough.

When I finally caught up to them, I saw Toby with his gun raised, and my father standing a few paces behind him, grunting *Shoo! Shoo, goddamn it!* I looked around for whatever it was he seemed to be trying to chase away, but all I could see was the buck collapsed on the ground, blood pouring from one of its back flanks. Then I realized my father was yelling at Toby to shoot.

The buck twisted its head around, black eyes running tears, horns bent forward, menacing, and Toby shot. The buck shrieked in pain, an impossibly high sound, like a whistle. Toby fell to his knees, screaming.

My father turned to me then and watched as I raised my gun, bracing myself as he'd taught me. The buck, meanwhile, struggled to stand. When I shot, its whole body jumped and a bubble of blood burst from its mouth and nose. It convulsed twice, and then it was dead. Its eyes rolled and fixed me with a look of such undiluted sadness that I had to turn away, even as my father ordered me to look back again, out of respect.

Almost immediately the buck's eyes clouded over. I had never seen anything so irrevocably dead in all my life.

A few moments later my father came toward me, awkward in his hunting boots.

"Good boy," he said, "good job."

At that moment, however, I couldn't have cared less what he thought. I didn't want his praise, I didn't want his blessing. What I really wanted just then was to go off alone somewhere and cry—though I wasn't sure whether it was because I'd killed something or because everything my mother had said about my father had turned out to be true.

Perhaps my father read my confusion and was disappointed. Perhaps he missed it altogether. In any case, he backed away from me slightly, then turned quickly and stamped back through the stiff grass and dipped his fingers in the deer's blood. He returned to where I was standing and drew a line across my forehead; then he did the same thing to Toby.

"Mark of the hunter," he said, standing there with one hand on his hip and the other holding his gun in the air. He whooped. I whooped too, imitating him, and raised my free hand in a fist. Toby smiled and made a weaker noise, clogged with phlegm.

My father wiped his hand on his trouser leg. "Well now, how's that for exciting, boys?" he asked. "Y'uns just have to learn to kill a little cleaner is all."

Afterward, we hauled the deer through the woods and dumped its carcass in the back of the truck, a foolish thing now, its antlers butting up against the back window. When we got home, my father would saw them off and mount them on a plaque with the date carved below, adding it to the collection he kept in the basement. The deer would become a story: my first kill. I imagined him telling it for years, long after Toby and I were grown.

I rolled down my window and leaned my head outside to feel the wind rush through my hair, until my father yelled across the cab for me to pull my head back in before it got clipped by a damn telephone pole.

My mother, nearly blind with a hangover, was still in her bathrobe when we got home. Her hair was dirty and snarled, and her face looked like crushed petals. She didn't approve of hunting, and when she saw me marked with the signs of my first kill, she closed her eyes and shuddered.

"Wash your hands," she said. "There's blood all over you." Then she turned away, walked back to her room, and emphatically shut the door.

My father told me not to bother cleaning up because we still had work to do. With Toby's help, we hauled the deer out of the back of the truck and into the front yard. My grandmother, wearing one of my grandfather's wool hunting jackets, came out to join us. She knelt on the ground, working with her knife, her hands, helping my father gut and slice the deer; dropping pieces of bloody meat into the buckets Toby and I carried between the front yard and the basement. When the butchering was through, Toby and I brought out the garden house to spray down the truck, wiping it down fast before the water had a chance to freeze. Cold numbed our fingers and made us clumsy.

"I'm gonna get ten more deer before the season's over," Toby announced, teeth chattering. He mimed aiming and shooting a rifle. "Right between the eyes."

Meanwhile, a foamy red slush collected in the gutter and more in the yard when we sprayed it down. I watched it sink into the ground, seeing rivers of blood flow where people all over the county were cutting up their kill: streams of it, feeding the earth through the long winter. And come spring, flowers opening out like dirty hands.

"Best damn fun I ever had," Toby said.

My father's other hobby was fishing, and accompanying him on trips to Potter Lake was only marginally more pleasant than hunting. Far worse than the awkward silence that usually hung between us, was the life jacket I had to wear, a bulky orange thing that made my arms look pathetically thin.

No matter how much I begged, my father wouldn't let me drive the boat. "You run over a rock," he told me, "you'd tear the bottom right out this here thing. Then where'd you be at?"

He'd go out by himself, though, sometimes staying out past dark. These nightly disappearances unnerved my mother, and fueled her suspicions that he was angling for other things besides fish. She would drink more than usual on the nights he stayed out late.

Three weeks after my eleventh birthday, I came home breathless and sweaty after a touch football game in the schoolyard. My legs were red with mosquito bites, and I had a scrape on my arm nearly five inches long. July was drawing to an end and the days were already getting shorter; nights came on suddenly, purple and humid, punctuated by weary grown-up voices calling their children home.

The first thing I noticed was the number of cars lined up in front of my grandmother's house. As soon as I came into the yard, Mrs. Hewitt ran out the kitchen door to stop me, pinching the flesh of my upper arm and asking in a grating whisper where the hell I'd been, and why didn't I come home when I heard people shouting for me.

Before I could even answer, she started rubbing my face and arms with the flap of her apron, and brushing my hair with her fingers. When Toby came over from the sidewalk and asked what was going on, his mother told him to stay in his own plate and get home quick if he didn't want a whipping.

Then she did something even stranger. She knelt on the grass and put her arms around my waist. Tears slid past the rims of her glasses as she told me I had to be strong, and good, because my father's boat had been found overturned in the lake and nobody knew where he was.

Curiously enough, the news didn't fill me with grief or fear or misgiving. It didn't fill me with anything at all.

I felt altogether emptied by it.

It was dark inside the kitchen. Once my eyes adjusted to the change I saw my mother sitting at the kitchen table between her oldest brother and his wife—Uncle Patrick and Aunt Mary. Their daughter, my cousin Judith, stood against the far wall, looking down at the floor. Neighbors crowded around the room and in the parlor, and the kitchen counter was piled with platters of food they had brought. My grandmother sat by herself, waiting beside the telephone.

As soon as I entered the kitchen my mother began to sob, and I slid past Uncle Patrick and put my arms around her while she cried into my chest. When I pulled away, there was a wet ring where she'd pressed her mouth against my shirt. Mrs. Pulaski, wearing a pink blouse and a headband, set a plate of ham and baked beans in front of me.

We waited a long time for news. Around ten o'clock, the phone rang. My grandmother answered, speaking in a low voice to the person on the other end and nodding occasionally. After she hung up, she told us that the sheriff had decided to call off the search until morning. It took a few moments for everyone to absorb the implications of the sheriff's decision. Gradually, the women closest to the counter started covering the food and finding places for it in the refrigerator, and over the next half hour or so the friends, family, and neighbors filed out.

When everyone was gone, my mother went to the cupboard and pulled out a bottle of scotch.

"I can drink if I want to," she said, to no one in particular.

My grandmother and I sat listening to her feet slapping on the floor as she went down the hall to her bedroom, and then her door slammed. My grandmother stood up and took a glass from the drainer by the sink.

"Go on," she said, holding out the glass to me. "She shouldn't drink out the bottle."

As I took the glass from her, I saw for the first time that she wasn't wearing her religious medallion. We looked at each other for probably a second or two—barely more than a glimpse, like watching someone walk past a window before pulling the shade down. Then I took the glass from her and walked down the hall to my mother's room.

My father's body was never found, so a month after the accident, Father Wood said his funeral over an empty grave. My mother almost refused to go, having convinced herself that he was not dead but had actually run off with another woman. Only the combined efforts of my Uncle Patrick and Uncle Ames succeeded in persuading her to come to the cemetery. If he were dead, they reasoned, she'd at least have the comfort of knowing she'd paid him proper respect. If he weren't, then he'd have to bear the greater onus of causing her so much unjustified grief.

The idea of looking blameless appealed to my mother.

Toby Hewitt, Dana Pulaski, Charlie Holubeck, and several other neighborhood boys came to the grave site with their parents. They stood together in a small group, a few feet apart from the rest of the mourners. After the funeral, their fathers shook my hand and told me to look out for my mother and grandmother now. Their mothers for the most part patted me sympathetically on the shoulder. Mrs. Pulaski bent and kissed me, leaving a thin shred of her perfume on my cheek. Dana stepped up afterward and shook my hand as seriously and gravely as his father had.

"See you," he said, looking me in the eye.

It was a simple thing to say, and I appreciated his sincerity. The rest of my friends had seemed either embarrassed or grateful to get away. As if losing my father in such an odd, unfinished way represented some sort of vaguely unpleasant liability.

As I watched them all head off in one direction, my family began moving away in another toward their own cars. For a few seconds I found myself standing alone among the gravestones, lost, confused, and not a little angry.

One week after the funeral my mother expended whatever good credit her recent widowhood had earned her. It was early evening, and several neighbors were taking the air on their front porches after dinner. A number of neighborhood children were playing in their front yards.

Riotously drunk, my mother bolted out the front door of my grandmother's house and stumbled sobbing and moaning incoherently toward the road. As she reached the curb, a truck came roaring down at her, horn blaring. My mother froze, throwing her arms in front of her face, like a nymph changing to the likeness of a tree. The truck disappeared around the corner, narrowly missing her. She collapsed in a heap on the side of the road, babbling.

Neighbors came out off the porches to stare and shake their heads, some pitying my mother and some my grandmother, who had come outside by then, too. Curiously, no one crossed the street to offer any help. I sensed in their reluctance the same sort of embarrassment I'd felt from my friends at the grave site. As though my father's death and my mother's response made other people uncomfortable, like a bad smell that would be rude to point out.

My grandmother and I hoisted my mother by her armpits and walked her back inside the house. She sat limply in one of the kitchen chairs, a thread of blood dangling from a cut on her cheek, a thread of spit from the corner of her mouth. Though she stank of bourbon, it wasn't the liquor that made her run, but rather the slow, steady accumulation of knowing that my father wasn't coming home anymore; that the accident itself had only been a messenger of a death still to come in the form of an empty chair, a door not banging open, a pillow losing its scent. These small absences made up his real death, a tardy guest who stayed and stayed.

After this incident, my mother began spending more and more time alone in her room. Uncle Patrick and his wife visited regularly, and every once in a while managed to cajole her into seeing a movie or having dinner at their house. Every few weeks, Uncle Ames drove over from Columbus. But as my mother disappeared further behind an alcoholic pall, the visits became less frequent.

Periodically, she would erupt into fits of temper or grief, and occasionally she'd pass out in the hallway or the bathroom or the kitchen. For the most part, she was so quiet it was easy to forget that she lived in the same house with us. When people asked how she was doing, we usually told them she was sick.

In the fall, my grandmother took a second job. In addition to her housecleaning work, which she managed to shift to the weekends, she worked five days a week behind the candy counter at a five-and-ten in Fairview, the largest town in the county. She came home every evening at 6:30—later if she stopped along the way for groceries—pushing open the door of the old white and turquoise Ford she drove and lifting out her feet one by one. Her ankles were often swollen to twice or three times their normal size. After eight hours on her feet dispensing mints, nonpareils, and jujubes to all manner of local residents, she tended to move more slowly than usual.

With my grandmother away from home most of the day and my mother hiding in her room, I had, in a sense, been granted every child's fantasy: a life without supervision. Unfortunately, I lacked the initiative to take advantage of my relative freedom. Embarrassed by the judgment I felt hanging over my family, I found it increasingly difficult to spend time around other people. I imagined looks passing between my friends, and slurs that might not actually have been made. As a result, I spent more and more time by myself. I pretended I wasn't home when Toby or Dana or Charlie came to the front door looking for me, and made excuses when they caught up with me. I told them I had to stay home because my mother was sick.

I spent a lot of time imagining that my father wasn't really dead. Some of the scenarios I invented were quite elaborate. For instance, I imagined him suddenly stepping from behind one of the trees by the side of the road as I made my way home from school—or perhaps I'd hear him call my name first. He'd tell me not to come any closer, and when I asked why, he'd explain that if he showed himself, we'd all be in terrible danger. Then he'd describe a place where he'd buried a box of thousand-dollar bills, which I was supposed to dig up and take home to my mother, along with a message that varied, but always included that he loved her, and would join us soon, and everything would be much better than it had been before.

After a while I began to lose track of where these fantasies left off and simple facts—like getting up and going to school, coming home to dinner and homework, going to bed, and starting the whole round over again the next day—began. Then I'd find myself on the side of the Route 9 staring off into the trees without knowing how long I'd been standing there. Or bolting out of bed for no apparent reason. Or standing downstairs in the kitchen with no clothes on, in the middle of the night.

At least once a month I rode my bike down to Potter Lake and skipped a stone over the water. I couldn't say for sure if I kept this up because I thought I'd see my father's hand reach up out of the water and catch it, or because I hoped the weight of all those stones would keep him down for good.

Almost a year after the accident, I noticed a boy about my own age standing on a flat rock jutting out of the water twenty yards from shore. People often used it as a diving platform. I watched him draw his arms over his head, arch his body, and plunge headfirst into the water. I watched, waiting, for a solid minute, and when he didn't come up I kicked off my shoes, preparing to swim in after him.

Abruptly, he resurfaced closer to shore, spitting water out of his mouth. He waved, waiting to see if I'd join him or go about my business, and when I didn't move he simply swam away.

I didn't learn his name until two weeks later, when I went with my grandmother to visit some people that had just moved into town. We'd left my mother at home in bed, quietly nursing a bottle of Jack Daniels.

My grandmother had baked a cherry roll for the occasion, and it was my job to carry it. I was so preoccupied with brushing bees away from the cherry roll that I all but forgot my resentment at having to spend a perfectly hot summer day indoors eating stale cookies and answering polite questions about myself. When we reached the bottom of the hill, my grandmother stopped to pull a handkerchief out of her sleeve.

"You know Alabama?" she asked, wiping her face. "Where it's at?"

I nodded.

"That's where Mrs. Paley come up from," she said.

"Uh-huh."

"She's born here though. Went to Alabama with her husband, and let the house to renters after her ma and pa passed. Now her husband's passed in the Vietnam."

We started walking again until we came to a fork in the road, then turned left down an unpaved street until we reached a two-story white house with green shutters. A rose of Sharon tree stood in the front yard, bursting with flowers the color of scars; and poplars rose along the back of the house, tall soldiers in green and silver uniforms.

Mrs. Paley's house smelled of eucalyptus, and every room was carpeted, even the kitchen. The tables in the parlor were made of a pale yellow wood, and the couch and chairs shared the same, boxy shape. Mrs. Paley informed us that the style was Danish modern. My grandmother nodded admiringly and then glanced at me and rolled her eyes.

Mrs. Paley's face seemed to be paralyzed in an attitude of perpetual surprise: eyes wide, mouth in the shape of an O. While we sat in the kitchen drinking Cokes, she kept asking me questions, calling me *honey,* and *lamb,* and *you-all.* Her attention made me so uncomfortable I eventually excused myself to go hide in the bathroom.

My real intention, however, was to take a closer look at what seemed to be a shrine of some sort in the far end of the parlor. I wasn't quite sure what I expected; maybe a bone or a tongue, like the ones in the churches in Europe that my sixth-grade teacher, Sister Sophia, enjoyed describing. In fact, the object turned out to be a purple heart, laid out on a pillow under a glass bell.

While I stood there tracing my finger over the glass, a voice came from behind me.

"You want to touch it?"

I turned around to see the boy from the lake standing right behind me. I hadn't even heard him approach.

"I didn't touch anything," I told him.

"Never said you did," he replied. "I asked did you want to."

He was shirtless, his skin burned brown by a sun whose heat I could only guess at. His hair was bleached the color of straw.

"Go on," he said, stepping past me and lifting the glass bell. "It's mine, so I got as good a right as anybody let you touch it."

He tugged the medal off the pillow and held it by the ribbon between his thumb and forefinger. I caught it just as he let it drop into my open palm.

"Just an old piece of metal," he continued. "Nothin' more than that."

"It belonged to your dad, didn't it?"

The boy stepped closer, so that our arms touched and I could feel the heat snaking off his skin. He plucked the medal out of my hand and let it dangle in midair.

"I never knowed him. He was always over there."

"Where?"

He named a number of peculiar sounding places while swinging the medal back and forth.

"You want it?" he asked.

"It's not yours."

Regardless of the truth of my observation, he pressed it into my hand. "I want you to have it," he said, lowering his voice and pushing his face close to mine. "I'll tell my mom I lost it. I'll tell her I was playing with it outside."

"Won't you get strapped?"

"Maybe."

We stood close together while he cupped my hand, squeezing the fingers shut.

"She couldn't wait to get out of that swamphole my daddy drug her down to," he said.

I glanced down at a corner of the ribbon poking out the edge, then back up at his wise, lopsided grin. His gaze, at once frank and slightly weary, seemed to draw a circle around us, a knowledge of adult things that only we two shared. He waited for my response. Admission to this circle required an exchange of confidence of similar value.

So I told him that my mother got drunk every day.

He nodded as if confirming something he'd already known.

A moment later, Mrs. Paley called my name, and the boy gestured for me to hide the medal in my pocket. He stepped ahead of me into the kitchen and threw his arms around his mother's neck. She smiled up at him from her chair and said his name, *Reis*: Like the morning sun, rise and shine.

Mother and son resembled each other quite closely at first glance, with their blond hair and muddy, green eyes. But whereas Mrs. Paley's face had a roundish, flattish shape, Reis looked more like a hungry cat. Mobile, tense, full of angles.

I felt a quick stab of jealousy, watching them together. Reis kept one arm around his mother's shoulder while he ate a forkful of cherry roll off her plate. After he pronounced it *de-licious,* my grandmother asked him if he wanted a piece of his own. He nodded, licking the fork with a loud smacking sound, at which his mother laughed and slapped him lightly on the arm.

"Mind your manners, sir," she said.

My grandmother cut a piece for each of us, and as we sat across from each other at the table to eat, she asked him how he liked Ohio. Reis replied that he liked it well enough; it wasn't as godawful hot as Alabama, and the mosquitoes weren't as big as crocodiles.

Then my grandmother and Mrs. Paley went back to talking about who had died since Mrs. Paley had lived in town, and who had gotten married, and after enough of that Reis and I excused ourselves and went out to the backyard, where we spent the next hour running back and forth playing a game of tag.

Mrs. Paley called out once from the kitchen window, asking us to please not trample the garden. It hardly looked worth worrying about—only a few spidery roses and some half-dead bushes—but we were careful all the same.

I believe it was Reis who broke into my grandmother's house at some point between the time she was found dead and the time I arrived. I believe he was looking for some sign of my whereabouts. Or perhaps, like one animal leaving its scent on another's territory, he wanted to let me know he'd been here. I can't offer any rational grounds to explain why I believe such a thing, only that it seems consistent with his style. If there's a more complicated way of doing something, Reis will be sure to try it.

After an uncomfortable first night in my grandmother's house, I wake to a coldness that feels unforgivable. City life has made me soft. To keep warm, I have to pull the blanket off the bed and wrap it around my shoulders as I trudge stiffly down to the kitchen to get some coffee into me. With any luck, my heart will start pumping after a couple of gulps.

Of course, it doesn't occur to me until I'm in the kitchen that there might not be any coffee—a possibility that begins to take on the dimensions of tragedy as I go through the cupboards one by one. Caffeine is one of the few vices I can still enjoy, and I don't like it in any form but coffee. The blanket keeps slipping off my shoulders and the linoleum chills my feet. Irritation snaps me more awake than I want to be.

At last, my search is rewarded with an old jar of instant coffee. I have to use a knife to loosen enough granules to make one weak cup. Sitting at the table to drink it, I look out the corner window, which frames a scene of nearly perfect white except for the trees that stand out like iron posts. The few houses I can make out from this vantage appear uncannily square, their edges vivid against the snow. It's the kind of scene that might fit nicely inside a glass paperweight, far cleaner and more vibrant than anything I remember from childhood. A feeling somewhere between giddiness and dizziness overwhelms me, but I hesitate to name it until it has already passed.

It's joy.

I wait till after the caffeine kicks in to look for the telephone book, the most reasonable place to begin an attempt to contact someone whose phone number you can't remember—who has, in all probability, changed residences over the past twenty-five years. After a search of the kitchen proves frustrating, I proceed to the hall closet, and then the smaller closet in the laundry room. It's in none of these places, naturally, so I move farther afield, searching my grandmother's bedroom, even getting down on my hands and knees to look under the bed.

It turns up, finally, under the sofa, propping up one corner where the wooden leg had broken off. As I pull the phone book out, the sofa tilts at a slight angle that looks vaguely like a sardonic smile. Quickly now, I thumb through the book to the *P*'s. Though there are a number of listings under Paley, I can't see anything for Reis or for Roberta, his mother. There's not even an R. Paley.

I don't know why I expected it to be easy.

Another, somewhat less protracted search uncovers my grandmother's address book behind the cookie jar next to the stove. Which makes me unaccountably happy. Most people organize their belongings in a moderately idiosyncratic manner, of course, and I wonder briefly if I'll find her checkbook in the freezer, or her keys in the washing machine. Probably not, but for an instant my grandmother is more alive in the little things she took for granted than in all my memories combined.

Unfortunately, the Paley's telephone number and address have been crossed out—which could mean any number of things. They could have moved to a different town, for example. Roberta may have died. There could have been some sort of rift or falling out. My grandmother may have simply forgotten to write in a new number for them, which could be scrawled on a scrap of paper anywhere in the house.

In any event, I'm surprised much less by my irritation over encountering setbacks than by the strong undercurrent of relief they cause. Though not an optimist by nature, I'm content to see these obstacles as a temporary reprieve.

It must have snowed again during the night, because ice grips my car windshield like barnacles, while the roof wears a white, felty sort of fez. It's a light, powdery snow, so the footprints cutting across the front yard are fairly easy to make out, one set leading toward the house, the other set leading away. The air is bright and crisp, like a tonic; a clarity so fragile I could crack it with a swat of my hand.

Even so, it takes a few moments for my brain to compute that someone besides myself must have made the footprints.

Cold air saws my lungs as I chip the ice off my windshield with the cheap plastic tool supplied by the car-rental company. My breath explodes in dense, white clouds. I have to stop twice to rest, leaning against the car to stare out over the snow blanketing old drifts and trees. Wondering if anyone is hiding nearby, watching.

Fairview, the largest town in the county, is fifteen miles north of Amity. Sure enough, on Main Street, there's a diner tucked between two brick buildings that look like they've been restored recently. The fronts are the color of fresh clay. I turn a corner and coast downhill to the lot. As I walk back up the hill the wind all but flays me open, easily penetrating the few layers of citified protection I've got on.

A bell trills as I enter the diner, and again when the door swings shut behind me. I'm greeted by the smell of fried bacon and old cigarette smoke, and from somewhere the sound of water running. Except for one old man sitting alone by the window, the place is empty. My fellow patron looks up when I come in and, without acknowledging me one way or the other, goes right back to staring out the window at the traffic of people in boots and heavy coats, and cars crawling down the street.

I pick a table near the back, near the bathroom, which has a paper sign on the door with the words MEN TOILET spelled out in black magic maker. The tablecloth seems to be an ancient species of vinyl, cracked and dirty, teeming with unpleasant things I know I shouldn't think about, but somehow can't resist imagining. A mound of cigarette butts fills the tin ashtray in the middle of the table. The menu, a torn, plastic covered affair that appears only marginally less infectious than the tablecloth, stands propped between a set of salt and pepper shakers and a bruised aluminum napkin holder.

After a minute, the noise of water stops and a gray-haired woman wearing a beige sweater over her uniform comes out of the kitchen to stand behind the counter. She shouts across the restaurant to ask if I want any coffee, and I nod yes, watching her pull together the cup, saucer, and spoon. She seems to list from side to side as she goes about getting my coffee, as if she's walking on a slanted floor.

When she comes around the counter and makes her way toward me, it's obvious she has a bad limp. I wonder whether she was born with this affliction or acquired it later, and how it affects the way she sees the world. It's a professional habit that rises almost automatically inside my head. The trick is to avoid getting too involved in what I'm thinking unless the situation demands it.

The waitress puts the cup down in front of me, hitches up her sweater, and pulls a pad and pencil from her skirt pocket.

"Know what you want?" she asks.

"What do you recommend?"

"Dunno honey, depends how hungry you are."

"Starving."

"Most people come in, they order the special," she tells me. "That's coffee and two eggs the way you like them, potatoes and toast." She sniffs. "And bacon. Cook's real good with it, makes it crispy without it being burned."

"That's what I'll have, then."

"How you want them eggs?"

"Scrambled, I think. Please."

She scribbles on her pad and then tilts her head a little to one side.

"Visiting or passing through?"

I shrug. "A little of both, I'd say."

"That so?"

"I used to live around here."

"I thought I recognized a face."

"It was more than twenty years ago."

"Honey, that's as far back and more as I lived here. Where was you living at?"

"Amity."

"Mostly Polish there."

"My grandmother was Polish. My grandfather was Czech."

"That so? I had an uncle was a bohunk." She smiles suddenly, showing the dull blank space where she's lost several teeth. *Summer teeth,* my mother used to call them: *some'r there, some'r not.*

The waitress leans a little closer to me, familiar now. "Sure picked a cold time to visit, huh?"

"My grandmother passed away. I came to clear out her house."

"That's too bad. Was she old?"

"In her seventies."

"Young. What was her name?"

"Julia. Julia Fowler."

The waitress, who now seems to have adopted me, squints and purses her lips. "Nope. Don't say as I know her, and I'm awful good at faces."

"She was pretty self-sufficient," I reply. "She didn't eat out much."

"Still."

I hesitate a few seconds before saying, "Maybe you can help with something else. I'm looking for an old friend."

"That so?"

"It's possible he may still live around here."

She sidles closer to the table and rests a hand on her hip. I can feel my face go warm under her look.

"His name is Reis Paley," I say.

She thinks a moment, frowning, and I feel my chest getting tighter, constricting my breath. My heart beats faster, thumping.

"Na," she says, shaking her head. "Can't say as I know him."

Once more, the feeling of reprieve washes over me, although the relief is cut short by a burst of wind rattling the front window. We both turn to watch a garbage can rolling down the street, and a man wearing a long white apron over his down vest chasing after it. Then the waitress turns back around.

"Day'll come that window blows in and that'll be a good mess." She tears a slip off her pad, shakes her head, and smiles again. "Lemme get this in, afore you starve to death."

I finish my coffee in three gulps. It's not as strong as I like it, but it's coffee all the same. Like a true addict, I relish every synaptic flutter.

I pick up a paper abandoned on the table next to mine, and flip through the pages, reading about the winter graduates from the university; the ten people arrested over the past week for driving while intoxicated; the woman who had opened a beauty parlor in her home; another who'd lost her food stamps in the grocery store.

A few minutes later, the waitress comes back with my food, and as I look up to thank her, I notice the old man at the front of the diner staring in my direction. His bald head shakes, like an egg perched delicately on top of his humped shoulders, but I can't tell if he's nodding at me or merely shivering. Out of politeness, I smile back at him before turning to my food and the rest of the paper.

After I finish eating and pay my bill, the old man waves to me. I don't want to be rude, so I go over to him. He leans toward me and asks, in a wavering voice, if I'm looking for Reis Paley. I reply that I am.

"He's gone," he says, shaking his head.

I have to swallow suddenly.

"He's gone? Do you mean he died?"

"Na." The old man laughs, or wheezes maybe. A wet, unpleasant sound. "Gone. Left town."

"Do you remember when that was?"

"Ya sure, it was years ago." He nods now, as if satisfied with his recollection, and then bends closer to me. I can smell coffee on his breath, and something else, the smell of old flesh. "He set fire to that old barn over there in Amity, you know where that was?"

Unless there were two barns in Amity that happened to catch fire under mysterious circumstances, he means the one that used to look down over my grandmother's street. It's unsettling enough that the event seems to have entered in some small way into the store of local trivia. It's even more disturbing to hear that Reis was blamed for setting the fire.

Attempting to sound noncommittal, I merely tell the old man that I know the place.

He wheezes again. "Set fire to the barn and skipped town the same night, nobody seen a bit of him since. Has people here though, but I don't say as they know any where he is, neither. What you want him for?"

"He was a friend of mine."

The old man pulls back a bit, squinting. "Can't see as I'd put the two of y'uns together."

"It was a long time ago," I reply, lightly apologetic.

"Ya, well, he's gone and good riddance, we don't need any more of that sort around here. There's enough troubles these days already."

In an attempt to end the conversation, I agree with him that the world seems more complicated than when I was young, and then head awkwardly for the door. Outside, I find myself breathing hard, expending far more effort than the frigid weather demands. As I reach the parking lot, I realize that the exertion has nothing to do with the cold. I'm angry at my pathetic attempt to excuse my friendship with Reis. But who am I angry at? Myself or the old man?

After thinking about it for a while, I'm less interested in the idea of Reis starting the fire in the barn than by the news that he left town the same night I did. Of course, it's possible the old man simply got us mixed up. A stranger could easily have mistaken us as boys. We were about the same height, the same build and coloring. And we were almost always together.

The summer I became acquainted with Reis had begun momentously for a number of reasons. Chief among them, of course, was my successful campaign to convince my grandmother to get me a pair of bell-bottom pants for my thirteenth birthday. Although departures from the sartorial norm were forbidden at Mother of Sorrows School, a number of my classmates had already taken to wearing unconventional items outside of school. Dana Pulaski, for example, had a suede vest with three-inch fringes along the bottom and pockets. Charlie Holubeck wore a big plastic peace symbol on a cord around his neck.

What we wore was tame compared to the odd assortment of ponchos, patches, sandals, and headbands on display when a group of hippies collected in Fairview to protest the war in Vietnam. Some of my friends' parents said it was a sin that young people should behave in such an unpatriotic manner when American soldiers were dying for democracy half a world away. Others sided with the protesters, saying there was no reason for us to be over there in the first place. The disagreements sometimes grew quite intense as angry voices pierced the thick air of summer nights. Certain names and phrases were uttered with dread or accusation. *Kent State. Black Panthers.*

Almost all the adults I knew agreed, however, that there were worse problems than hippies. Even in our sheltered corner of Ohio, the kinds of people my mother used to call delinquents were smoking stronger things than Trues or Marlboros. Nor were they content to loiter in back of the grocery store or the schoolyard.

Just before school let out for the summer, an entire family had been found murdered ten miles away from Amity in Egypt Bottom, a valley choked with weeds and scrub that served to conceal an untold number of rusted out trailers and rickety shacks cobbled together from the corrugated metal, and the sides of discarded washing machines, and pieces of other shacks that had long since collapsed. One of the people who found the bodies said every member of the family had deep gashes across their necks that looked like black mouths, crawling with flies. Many county residents automatically assumed that the killer, who was never found, must have been a drug addict. Common knowledge at the time held that all drug addicts were homicidal maniacs.

Such atrocities weren't supposed to happen in rural Ohio, where most people never even considered locking their doors or windows at night, and the fact that such a grisly act occurred sent a wave of unease through the general population. Over the course of that summer, Putnam County seemed to become a more dangerous and distrusting corner of the world.

My acquaintance with Reis, meanwhile, unfolded as a kind of courtship, a dance in which neither partner felt quite brave enough to take the lead. We rode around on our bicycles with no destination in mind, just to get away. To an empty field sometimes, or the woods, or Potter Lake. Sometimes we followed the railroad tracks, picking black raspberries that grew wild there, until the sun went down, blood orange behind the hills, and lightning bugs flickered around our heads.

Nights, we'd camp out on an old slate dump west of town, hardly sleeping, the drawl of our boyish voices riding the warm night air until the moon sank in the west. Whenever Toby or any of my other friends asked me to go swimming or join them in a game, I lied and said my mother was sick or that my grandmother needed me at home.

On the first anniversary of my father's death, Reis and I spent the afternoon at the creek that ran through the meadow below the barn. The water was deep and cool under the willows, and after lounging in the water for about half an hour we stretched out head to head in the sun, completely enfolded in the rough, metallic smell of weeds and the murmur of bees. After a while, I asked Reis if he ever thought about his father.

"Told you I never knowed him," he replied.

"I mean fighting in the war and all. Bombs, and getting shot at. How did he die?"

"In a plane."

"Was he the pilot?"

"He was in the plane."

"He wasn't the pilot, then."

"My mom says he was a spy."

"That's something."

Reis flicked a black ant off his shoulder. "Sure," he said. "People back home said he was a genius."

"What do you think?"

"I know it for a fact."

"How?"

"He just had to be, don't you see?"

"Nope."

"Well, what do you know anyway?"

He lay quietly a little longer, then sat up on his elbows.

"Let's get out of here," he said. "I'm burning." He went a few yards before turning back. "What you waiting for?"

"Just laying here," I replied softly. "Like a lazy old dog."

I hardly moved, afraid Reis could read my thoughts the same way he'd been able to know that I'd coveted the purple heart medal in his mother's living room.

The truth of the matter was, I wasn't sorry my father was dead. On the contrary, I was secretly relieved. And though I was fairly confident that Reis felt the same way about his own father, I wanted to hear him to say so straight out. It would have gone a long way toward relieving the burden of dread and confusion hanging over me.

As it was, I was half convinced that something was seriously wrong with me. Father Fernando, the Cuban refugee priest who gave religious instruction at Mother of Sorrows on Wednesdays and Fridays, made it very clear where God stood on such matters as respect for one's parents.

In a voice become prematurely raspy after the removal of a cancerous lump from his throat, he explained that the problem with the world today was that too many children ignored the fifth commandment to honor their fathers and mothers. As a direct result, they descended into a life of sin and degradation—which included, among other horrors, drug addiction, abortion, adultery, homosexuality, murder, and pornography—from which it was almost impossible to rise up again and at the end of which yawned the never-ending agony of the flames of hell.

Instead of providing the direct answer I was hoping for, however, Reis merely conceded that I was a lazy old dog. He added further that I was welcome to go home with him for a tall, cool glass of lemonade from the pitcher his mother had made up fresh that morning, but that he wasn't going to stand there under the hot sun, waiting forever. And since there didn't seem to be much point in laying out in the meadow all by myself, I decided to take him up on his offer.

I stayed at his house much longer than I'd expected, since, as it happened, NASA had chosen the anniversary of my father's death to land the *Apollo 11* astronauts on the moon. I stayed for dinner, and afterward sat with Reis and his mother in their living room, staring at the blue-gray images displayed on an old Zenith black-and-white television screen. I have to say that the significance of the event was lost on me, and I didn't quite understand why Roberta started crying when the first astronaut said something about steps, or why she insisted that Reis run and get the Brownie camera from the hall closet so she could take a picture of the television screen.

To my mind, the prospect of going to hell seemed a good deal more urgent than the idea of going to the Moon.

The only person who might know how to get in touch with Reis is my cousin Judith, and after leaving the diner in Fairview I drive to her house, which is about ten miles north, in Belmont.

She answers the door holding a plastic watering can in one hand and a bunch of yellowed leaves in the other. I haven't seen her since Uncle Ames died, when she came to Columbus for the funeral. She was already married by then, and busy raising two small boys. Six months later, I moved to New York.

"Christian," she says now, her voice high and breathy, but not unpleasant. "I wasn't sure you'd come."

"I hope this isn't a bad time?"

"No, please." She steps back to let me pass. "Come in."

I've brought her a package, a relic from my grandmother's house, wrapped rather clumsily in old newspaper. After stepping over the threshold, I set the package on the floor and simply stand awkwardly for a moment, wondering whether I should hug her or just take my coat off.

In those few seconds I can see that age has drawn an interesting quality out of her. Not beauty, precisely, but rather a kind of delicacy. Her cheeks are hollow and the skin over them is just beginning to sink; her neck is longer and thinner than I remember. There are other changes, too—lines in her face, a bit of gnarling in the hands. Her hair, once thick and very dark, is patchy now and streaked with gray. She's taken to wearing it short, which isn't the most becoming style for her face.

When we embrace, she feels like bundled sticks in my arms, so thin I'm afraid to hold her too tightly or too long. She insists on helping me off with my coat, and then points to a tray near the door where I can put my boots. While I sit on the stairs and slowly work my feet out of my boots, she whisks away to hang up my coat, returning before I've even gotten one foot free.

"When did you get into town?" she asks.

"Yesterday. Late."

"You're staying . . . ?"

"At my grandmother's."

"She'd find that a comfort."

"Maybe."

A smile flicks across her lips. "It's what you're supposed to say," she replies. "Not necessarily the truth. Is there going to be a funeral?"

"She never wanted one. Her ashes are at Chase funeral parlor."

To fill the silence, Judith asks if I'd like something to drink and goes ahead of me down the hall. She has a light walk, athletic, as if she's given up any need for seductiveness. In the kitchen, a white ceramic cross on one of the walls, and just below it, a cross-stitch plaque that reads GOD BLESS THIS HOUSE. Judith motions for me to sit while she digs in the refrigerator for something to drink. I put the gift I brought her on the table.

"How are your parents?" I ask.

"Fine, fine," she murmurs.

She straightens suddenly, and turns, clutching a bottle of root beer to her chest.

"What am I saying? Mom died two years ago. Dad's in a home."

"I'm sorry."

"Well. There you go."

She crosses to the cupboard, takes down a pair of glasses, and fills them with root beer. Then she comes to the table and sits across from me.

"I brought you something from Grandma's house," I say. "I remember you staring at it whenever you came over."

Judith studies the package.

"Go on," I insist. "Open it."

She takes her time pulling off the newspaper I'd wrapped it in, folding it into a neat square and setting it on the chair beside her. She stares down at her gift: a brass clock with an elaborate tangle of brass leaves around its face.

"Oh yes," she says, fingering one of the leaves. "I remember this. It was in the kitchen. I used to sit at the table watching the second hand go around and around while I held my breath. For hours, it seemed like."

"Why?"

"I don't know. To make the time go by. I couldn't stand those visits."

She laughs, a bright, hard sound, almost startling; then she pats my arm. The bones of her hand are close to the skin, no flesh at all on them. She sees me staring and pulls away.

"Let me show you around," she says.

The house, she informs me, is more than a hundred years old. The walls are mostly pale colors, pale peach, baby blue, and the furniture looks comfortable. While we're in the living room, she says she wishes I'd come back in time to see their Christmas tree in the front window.

"The boys went all out this year," she adds. "We weren't expecting to have Christmas together."

Her fingers do a nervous sort of dance on the back of a chair. I glance from that to a set of white plaster praying hands on the mantle. So far, every room we've been in has some type of icon in it—a cross, a tiny pietà, a miniature saint—each item unobtrusive in itself, but taken together suggesting more than casual devotion.

The most impressive specimen hangs in her bedroom: a large, gold-framed reproduction of a painting of Christ at Golgotha. From where I'm standing, I can't tell whether he's already dead or is still dying. In the agonized pose of crucifixion, his head droops backward at an awkward angle while his knees bend slightly in opposition; his arms are pinned wide along the beam of the cross. Except for the figure of Christ, everything in the painting looks dark and slightly sinister. The branches of surrounding trees are shaped like claws and the rocks in the background are gashed and splintered. Even the mourners look like a fairly desperate bunch, clumped together around the base of the cross.

It's not a very good painting, but the longer I look at it the more I'm drawn in by the twisted, half naked figure of the dying man, the mourners tearing at their clothes and hair. Even the little knot of soldiers in the corner, leaning idly on their spears, are fascinating in a grotesque sort of way.

At first I'm not sure what, precisely, has captured my attention. It's the light, I think, or maybe the starkness of the grief. Then, when I see what it really is, I'm tempted to deny any interest whatsoever.

Judith says nothing about the painting. Instead, she steps over to the dresser, motioning me to follow so she can show me the photographs arranged on it. She picks them up one by one, so I can appreciate them at close range while she explains them to me: the cottage on Lake Erie they rented one summer; her husband, David, on a snowmobile; her oldest son holding a trout he caught in a fishing contest; the younger boy at his high school prom.

They're a handsome family, and I tell her so.

"The boys are so grown up now," she replies. "I can hardly imagine the time going by so quickly. And I never even had to hold my breath."

"Where are they now?"

"In the mines, like their father."

She rearranges the pictures on the dresser.

"There's a strike on now, so they're probably down at the strike office, or picketing. Or drinking somewhere. It's hard on the younger men, nothing to do all day but get drunk and hate."

I remember strikes: the fights that broke out sometimes between the union workers and the scabs, police cars speeding down the road, and the feeling of importance, of event. My father had once come home with a broken nose. Judith was there that day—one of the dreaded visits to my grandmother's house—and when she saw my father, she turned white and ran out of the room with her hand over her mouth.

The sight of blood had always made her sick. At the public pool in Fairview, I tormented her once by slowly picking a scab off my knee. She must have been sixteen at the time, and I was twelve. I'd chased her halfway around the pool until the lifeguard made us stop. When we got back to our towels, she sat brooding, her dark hair hanging like raw silk in front of her face.

"It's just blood," I said. "You don't have to be such a baby about it."

"It's not the blood," she told me. "It's the fact that you did it. You don't do things to upset the people who love you," she informed me.

To which I replied that my grandmother said that people got stronger by seeing things they didn't like. Judith chose not to comment on this bit of wisdom, and turned over on her stomach to finish the book she was reading.

Later that afternoon, as we walked home from the pool, she took a detour through a field and stood me flat against a tree. I thought she was going to lecture me about the blood again. Instead, she pressed her mouth on mine and slid her tongue gently between my lips.

"That's the way to treat someone who loves you," she whispered.

The kiss hadn't lasted longer than a few seconds, but I remember walking out of the field feeling confused and a little frightened. I had an almost physical sensation of something unfolding inside of me, like a moth slowly unrolling its sticky wings for the first time. I'd never really considered bodies before, or the scary pleasures they could give and receive. Even so, as I contemplated the possibilities, I never considered kissing Judith again. She was my cousin; and for a long while that excuse seemed just as likely as any other.

Downstairs, Judith insists on making lunch. Something simple, she assures me: soup and sandwiches. She works quickly, efficiently, keeping up a steady stream of chatter about harmless things: the enormous new mall going up on Route 9, the junior high school that stands on some old farmer's orchard, the plans to revive the railroad that used to run through the county.

More than once I try to steer the conversation to the past, hoping to ease my way into asking about Reis. I suspect Judith knows this, and is making her best efforts to discourage me. She never cared for Reis when we were children.

"It's funny," she says once we're sitting in the dining room. "I used to think when the boys grew up, I'd enjoy having time to myself again. The peace and quiet, the chance to do all the things I said I was going to do."

"I remember you could finish a whole book in a single day."

"Oh yes. It's not the same. I don't think I've read a book in years."

She takes a long swallow of root beer and leans back in her chair.

"The truth is, I miss having babies around. They look you right in the eye and there's nothing hidden there, no lies, not even white ones. Nothing mysterious. When they need something, they cry, when they're happy, they laugh. When they're tired, they fall asleep." She takes another drink and smiles. "You know, you were my first baby."

"I beg your pardon?"

"That's the way I'll always think of you. I loved taking care of you when you were tiny, holding you, changing your diapers if your grandma was busy or your mom was sick."

"I believe drunk may be the word you're looking for."

"Don't speak ill of the dead. It doesn't do."

"That's right, you were always a good girl."

Judith shakes her head, laughing softly. "That girl is long gone, I think. I wonder where she went?"

Suddenly, her expression changes, and she points to the window behind me.

"A cardinal!"

She pushes her chair back and steps around the table to the window. I get up, too, and together we watch the bird rest a moment at a feeder in the middle of the backyard and then fly away: a flash of scarlet against the clouds. We don't go back to our seats right away, but just stand there, looking out at the snow.

"You know, that girl had a lot of silly ideas in her head," Judith says out of the stillness. "She saved herself up for a man who would speak sweetly to her, and when she couldn't find him she got scared and married the first man who asked. After all, she had to get married. She expected it. Who would she be if she didn't? So she bought a house and had a child and went to sleep."

"Forever?"

Judith bends her head to one side, as if appraising something. "Well," she says. "She did wake up once, when the man she might have waited for finally came along. But by then it was too late, there was a second child, a mortgage, a man who depended on her to take care of him. You think that was mistake, don't you?"

I don't know how to respond. I was fifteen when she got married; Judith was nineteen. She and her husband had seemed happy enough whenever they came to Columbus for a visit.

I tell her it's not a mistake if it was what she wanted.

"What I wanted," she replies. "Oh dear." She slides past me and goes over to a sideboard at the other end of the room. "I wonder if you should've come back, Chris? What do you hope to accomplish? The past looks after itself."

"I find that hard to believe."

"Sorry, that's what you do, isn't it? Dig up the past." Her tone is bright, still, but distracted. "What do they call it, the talking cure? That must be interesting."

She opens a drawer and fumbles though it until she finds a small white bottle. She unscrews the cap, bends her head back, and squeezes a couple of drops in each eye. She blinks a few times and then tilts her head back down.

"I had an operation last year," she says, looking straight at me. "We weren't sure I'd make it, but I did. Cancer. In the female parts. Excuse me."

She squeezes another drop in each eye, recaps the bottle, and returns it to the drawer.

Now, of course, the icons, the hints about Christmas and time passing too quickly and so on begin to make sense. I feel stupid for not picking up on the clues.

"The radiation dried my tear ducts and the membranes in my throat," she explained, "so I always have to be drinking something and putting these drops in. Can you imagine? What a bother." She wipes her face and dries her hand on a napkin before adding, "I went into a depression when I learned it was cancer."

"Did you see anyone about it?"

"Yes. Father Corerro, a charismatic who preaches up near Steubenville. He taught me to pray again after I'd forgotten how. He gave me absolution."

"For what?"

She leans back against the sideboard slowly shaking her head back and forth. A flush runs up her neck into her face and she starts to cough. It takes me a minute to realize that she isn't really coughing; she's making the sound someone who's been slow-burned from the inside would make when they're trying to cry.

"They cut me open, Chris," she says, shuddering. "They cut out my female parts."

I cross the room and put my arms around her shoulders. Her breath is on my neck, the moisture of artificial tears. After an instant of hesitation, she wraps her arms around me, tentatively at first, and then leaning into me.

We remain holding onto each other like that even after she stops crying: neither of us sure, apparently, how to treat the people who love us.

Much of what I know about loving, actually, I learned from Richard, whom I met only a month or two after I moved to New York. We met in a bar, which I hated, because after a few minutes I felt as though I were floating in a crowded fish tank. I drank my beer wedged against a wall, trying to find a blank space through all the bodies and cigarette smoke where I could stare without drawing any attention to myself. Then Richard moved into my line of sight.

"It's not really you," he said.

I had no idea what he meant until he brushed his finger across the mustache I was trying to grow.

"Sweet," he added. "But not you."

I thanked him, which, even as I was doing it struck me as a fairly asinine way to handle the situation. The men around us glanced out of the corners of their eyes. I thought they were smirking. Embarrassed, I kicked away from the wall and pushed through the crowd and out the door.

I walked home, which at the time was a tiny studio apartment in Hell's Kitchen. I wanted to erase Richard from my thoughts, so I dramatized his rudeness, his invasion of my body. There was only one problem: I'd liked the way his finger smelled when he ran it under my nose. I kept thinking about the way he looked, re-creating the details of his face. Gypsy eyes I told myself, to make the picture clearer. I used other words too, like *dark, swarthy*—not that he was either, particularly.

I shaved off my mustache as soon as I got upstairs to my apartment, but it took me two weeks to work up the courage to go back to the bar. My behavior wasn't much better the second time around. When Richard congratulated me on taking his advice about my mustache, I told him I hadn't shaved it off for his sake. Since he hadn't alluded to the possibility, I suppose I let slip a crucial bit of information.

"You're not from New York," Richard said.

"What do you mean?"

"Your accent."

I looked past him, at a knot of men by the bar. "I don't have an accent."

"Okay," he replied, smiling. "You don't sound like a New Yorker, how's that? So where are you from?"

"Ohio."

He waited. I still wonder why he didn't give up right then, when he saw how much work it was going to take.

"Look," he said finally, "you don't seem very comfortable here. Would you like to go somewhere less crowded?"

"I think I'd just like to leave," I said. "Thanks."

"Don't thank me." He put his hand on my arm. "Come and have a drink with me. A cup of coffee. A pizza."

"I can't." He was standing very close, and I could see the hurt in his face, so I added, "I have to get up early tomorrow."

"Tomorrow's Sunday."

"I have to go to church."

In fact, I did go to church the next morning: St Paul's, a gray stone building on the corner of Fifty-ninth Street, with two flights of stairs leading up to a set of massive wood doors, on either side of which stood a statue of a saint. I didn't go inside, though, but merely stood on the sidewalk, watching the families and couples going up the steps, greeting each other, adjusting their hats, stopping to tie their shoes.

That night, however, I went home with Richard. I don't remember if kissing him was pleasant or not, because I was too concerned over the fact that I was shaking—an embarrassing failure of nerve I hoped he would overlook. When we undressed, I was surprised how much smaller he looked without his clothes on; I'd almost say boyish, except that his body was covered in wiry, dark hair.

He was very kind. After a while, he asked me if I'd ever been with a man before.

"Yes," I replied.

Then, less defensively, "No."

Then finally, "Yes."

He didn't ask anything more, and he's never mentioned the difficult time I had that first night. Maybe he drew his own conclusions. Maybe, after a while, he simply forgot.

"The summer I broke my leg, do you remember?" Judith asks.

We're in the kitchen now. I'm making a pot of coffee while she cleans the lunch dishes.

"I cried almost every day for a month because I felt like such a goblin with that enormous cast on my leg. No one came around and I was convinced I would never have any friends for the rest of my life. But you came, every day on that funny little red bike that had been your mom's. You played cards with me and Chinese checkers and I don't remember what else."

"School. You gave me gold stars when I did well."

"That's right."

"There was a song you taught me," I say. "We had to sing it every time we went over the bridge to Wheeling. *The river is up, the channel is deep, the wind is steady and strong. . . .*"

"You remember that?" Judith laughs. "I used to get car sick unless there was something to distract me."

"I can't remember the rest of the words, though. *Oh Dinah something something something, as we go sailing along.*"

"Dinah put your hotcakes on."

"That's right. I remember now. I think I imagined her wearing them, like a hat. Dinah put your hotcakes on."

"Strange child."

I'm not sure how she means this remark—whether it's the closest she can come to acknowledging something she may find painful, embarrassing, or worse. Nevertheless, it may be the only opening she gives me and I decide to take it.

"Judith," I say, "I need to find Reis."

She opens her mouth to respond and then shuts it again and turns back to the sink.

"I don't know where he is," she replies.

"I looked in the telephone book this morning. It seemed as good a place as any to start. Actually, I didn't expect to find him listed, but I was surprised not to find anything for his mother. Did she go back to Alabama?"

"Roberta died five years ago. I guess your grandma didn't tell you."

The news stings, but I merely shake my head. Judith opens the cupboard below the sink, pulls out a dish towel, and starts to dry the dishes.

"I used to see Roberta in the grocery store sometimes," she says. "She was a nice woman, well-dressed, well-spoken. Lovely skin. Some women are lucky that way, you know, they never seem to age. I don't think she knew what to do with Reis."

"So you don't know how I could get in touch with him?"

"Coffee's ready," Judith says, moving past me toward the stove. "Do you take anything in it?"

"Milk. I'll get it."

She pours the coffee out while I reach the milk from the refrigerator. I add a splash to my cup and ask if she wants any, but she shakes her head no. She carries her cup to the table and sits. Pale afternoon light shining through the window softens her face. She looks like she might be praying.

"He came by looking for you right after your grandma died," she says. "I told him I hadn't seen you in almost twenty years. Which was the truth." She stirs her coffee, then takes a sip. "He's been in and out of prison for years, Christian. The last time was for trying to kill someone with his truck. He went halfway through the windshield."

"So he's still living here?" I ask.

"As far as I know."

"This morning someone told me he'd left town the night the barn burned down."

She shrugs.

"Someone broke into Grandma's house," I continue. "Smashed a window, made a mess of my room. Whoever it was left a footprint on my bed."

"Maybe he *should* have been the one to leave town that night," Judith replies.

"Maybe." I take a sip of coffee. "Maybe you're right, too, about the past taking care of itself. But if that's the case, then coming here isn't so much a choice I made as a consequence that I can't avoid."

"Clever." She smiles wanly. "But not smart."

After leaving Judith's, I drive to Potter Lake and park on a bluff overlooking the water. A dirt trail, choked with snow and ice at this time of year, winds down about twenty or thirty feet to the pebbly beach. The air seems warmer down by the water, or at any rate damper. A veil has collected over the water, part cloud, part fog.

Most of the stones along the shore are round or broken, and coated with a brittle veneer of ice that breaks away at a touch. It takes a while to find one flat enough, and when I throw it as far as I can out into the water, it skips only a couple of times before sinking.

I'm out of practice.

A set of footprints in the mud catches my eye; two sets, actually, a person's and a dog's. I stand there wondering what kind of dog it was, and what kind of person would match up with such and such an animal, until it occurs to me that the person and the dog might have come by at different times, and the mud simply froze the image of their separate passages.

As I turn to head back up to the car, I catch a glimpse of a man in a dark blue parka stepping abruptly away from the edge of the overlook.

When I reach the top, though, there's no one around; and mine seem to be the only tire tracks in the snow and the only footprints along the edge of the hill. It's possible that I didn't really see anyone at all, but that would be kidding myself. And now, in my head, I can hear Reis—the taunting, belligerent tone of a boy acting older than he was: *What are you afraid of?*

A week after I'd tried to draw Stephen out by talking about my own parents, he came back to my office, flopped down on the couch, and folded his skinny arms across his chest.

"So what's on for story hour today, Mister Rogers?" he muttered.

His hair was much shorter, almost a crew cut, and I mentioned the fact.

"Ya," he replied, "I'm thinking maybe I'll sign up for the marines."

"Seriously?"

He flashed a sardonic grin, as if he couldn't believe anyone would be so gullible. "Yeah, right," he said.

"I thought about it when I was your age."

"Bet I can guess why, too."

"I thought it would be an adventure."

"Right."

He wriggled on the couch until he found a more comfortable position. "So go on," he said. "Entertain me."

"You know, I'm getting tired of doing all the talking, Stephen," I replied. "Why don't you talk some?"

Stephen squinted and squeezed his arms closer to his chest. "Tricky, very tricky. Go on now. Once upon a time . . ."

I suppressed the urge to smile, and sighed instead.

"Alright," I began. "Once upon a time there was a therapist who had a really annoying patient. This patient had red hair and a nasty attitude—"

"Click."

"Excuse me?"

"Click. I'm changing the channel. That program was fucked up."

"Ah." I nodded, and then went on. "Anyway, this patient, it seemed, really liked holding out on everyone who tried to help him."

"Click."

"He wouldn't talk about what was going on inside his nasty little head—"

"Click. Click. Click."

"Sorry. I guess it's the same fucked up program on every channel."

I leaned back in my chair and clasped my hands behind my head. I was bluffing, of course, and if the ploy failed, I wasn't sure what I'd do. But I believed the potential advantages of teasing him outweighed the risks.

"Anyway," I continued, "this patient seemed to be more or less a blank slate. No memories, no stories, no events in his life. He never dreamed. Just an empty box. Dull, dull, dull."

For a few seconds, Stephen didn't move, didn't even blink. He simply sat with his arms squeezed across his chest. Then he muttered, "Don't shit me, doc. I'm your most interesting patient and you know it."

"Really?" I waited a few beats, giving measure for measure. "What would you say if I told you yes?"

The boy laughed, nervously, and glanced off to one side.

"Cut the crap," he said.

"No, seriously. If I told you that you were my most fascinating patient, and I looked forward to your visits more than anyone else's, would you believe me?"

He leaned his head against the back of the sofa, crossing his legs at the ankle. "You come on with all your patients this way, doc?" he asked.

"You think I'm flirting with you?"

"Yes sir."

I tapped my pencil a few times on the metal arm of my chair. It made a small and hollow sound, barely audible.

"What makes you think so?" I asked.

Stephen crossed and recrossed his legs, rubbed his nose, ran a hand through his hair. Then he grinned, an expression more of discomfort than pleasure.

"I mean look at yourself," he said. "Leaning back in your chair. The smile on your face. You're wanting me aren't you?"

"How would that make you feel if I were?"

"Ten points off. I asked you first."

I considered my options.

"I do want something," I replied cautiously, measuring my words. Seeking the right balance between honesty and encouragement. "I'm just not sure what it is, and you're the only one who can help me."

Stephen sat a moment chewing his lip. All at once, he pushed off the couch and ducked out the door so abruptly it might have been a magician's trick. I was left gaping in my chair, wondering if he would suddenly and just as magically reappear.

The following week, he arrived at his usual time and curled up as usual on the battered couch. And recounted a dream in which he found himself walking alone in a yellow field under a blue sky, feeling nothing, neither the heat nor the impression of corn stalks brushing against his body. The stalks parted for him as he passed among them.

I didn't recognize the dream as a retelling of his father's childhood experience of healing until he came to the part about seeing a tractor in the middle of the field. Almost immediately after mentioning it, though, he recanted a bit, saying maybe it wasn't a tractor. It was definitely a piece of farm machinery, though: an enormous metal contraption with heavy wheels. Red paint. It was tipped on its side and a man lay trapped beneath it, holding out his hand.

Touch me, the man begged.

And, in the dream, he did.

"See I got dreams, doc," Stephen said, at the end of his narration. "I got stories that would make you fucking weep."

After leaving Potter Lake, I head back south along Route 9 to the new Beuckman's grocery store, which is easily three times larger than the one I remember as a child. The old store had sold only groceries and perhaps a few stationery supplies. The new one has a bakery, a bank, a photo developing counter, and a video rental outlet. A banner outside the entrance announces future plans to add a garden shop, a pharmacy, and a food court. The produce aisles overflow with plump, luscious fruits and pimply, teenage boys in white shirts and aprons are busy repositioning packages of soap, cat litter, and paper towels so the shelves won't look empty.

Beuckman's grocery store has evolved into a suburban equivalent of heaven, where everything is readily available and nothing seems to die. Within five minutes, I'm exhausted by the sheer volume of choices. There's something desperate in the amount of items available, as though the pyramids of ripe cantaloupes and jumbo boxes of breakfast cereal had been precariously arranged to conceal some sort of grotesque, unpalatable truth. It's a relief to get back outside, to the simple clarity of snowdrifts and frigid air.

It's dark by the time I pull up in front of my grandmother's house. After unpacking the groceries and other household supplies, I return to the car for the boxes I found in a Dumpster at the back of the grocery store. Strong boxes, suitable for packing. I pile them against the far wall of the parlor.

On my way back to the kitchen, I grab the phone book off the parlor floor, and flip through the pages once again until I reach the listings for Paley. It's a long shot, but it can't hurt to try calling all the listings. Maybe one of them will turn out to be related to Reis, or at least be able to pass along some information about him.

After a few rings, a man picks up on the other end of the first number I dial.

"Reis?" I ask.

"What's that supposed to mean?"

"Ah." This is all I can manage for a couple of seconds. "I was looking for someone by the name of Reis Paley. I guess the operator gave me the wrong number."

"Guess so."

I can feel myself smiling stupidly, as if I'm actually facing the person on the other end. "You wouldn't happen to know him yourself would you? Or how I might get in touch with him?"

"You some sort of tax collector?"

"No, just a friend that's lost touch."

My stomach tightens.

"Afraid I can't help you, buddy," the man says.

"That's alright. I'm sorry to bother you."

"Yep."

I hang up and, before I lose my nerve, immediately dial the next number. I go down the whole list that way, talking to an old man, two women, and a child; none of them helpful. Two of the numbers haven't answered, so I copy their addresses on a scrap of paper. I don't recognize the street names, which means I'll have to get a map.

When I'm through, I have to go outside and stand on the front porch for a few minutes. It's starting to snow again, thick flakes sifting down through the yellow beams of the street lamps. Someone nearby has lit a fire and the smell of wood smoke fills the air. Without thinking, I find myself staring up at the bright knob of snow where the old barn used to be.

The fire had attracted quite a crowd. Some of the people had on only their bathrobes and pajamas. There were sirens and a lot of confusion. It's a good bet no one noticed me slipping out the back door and climbing over the backyard fence, following a back route along the creek that ran through the meadow.

Sometime after dawn, I crossed over to Route 9 and climbed in the ruined cab of a dusty truck that stopped at my thumb-out signal. The driver asked my name, and I told him. He said his name was Orin. He asked where I was headed, and when I told him Columbus, he replied that he wasn't going so far himself, but he could take me as far as New Athens.

It took six different rides to get to Columbus.

Uncle Ames had come to the door when I rang the bell. I reminded him that he'd told me at my father's funeral that if I ever needed a place to stay I should come to him. Naturally, he asked what had made me leave home.

"Nothing," I replied. "I just don't want to live there anymore."

That night I slept in a spare room in a bed with soft machine-dried sheets and feather pillows. Aunt Jane brought up a glass of milk and a plate of cookies, and stroked my forehead with cool fingers and said she was glad I'd come, it would be nice to have a child in the house. She wished me pleasant dreams as she left the room, and I sank into the atmosphere of cleanliness and calm, embracing sleep the same way a castaway might clutch the shore. Relieved and thankful, not bothering to ask how well I'd survived.

Back in the house, I make a quick dinner: a cheese omelette, toast, and salad. Afterward, I head down to the basement to look for a toolbox, which turns up in what used to be the fruit cellar, an alcove set off from the rest of the basement by a curtain. There are still jars of tomatoes, peaches, and a few less distinct varieties of produce sitting on the shelves, shrouded in dust. I pick one up and hold it to the light. Pickled melon rinds, gray with mold.

I carry the toolbox up to the parlor and set it down in front of the door. Seven nails hold the board in place—two at the top, two on each side, and one at the bottom. They squeal as I pull them out. I take the board down the hall to my parents' bedroom and nail it against the broken window.

When I'm done, I go back to the kitchen and pour a glass of wine. I don't really want to start packing, deciding what to keep, what to throw away. It feels too much like robbing a grave.

It's raining in the morning, a steady shower that pokes holes in the snow. Steam rises from the ground, and clouds cap the tops of even small hills. I drive until I find a gas station, which consists of two rusting pumps in front of a square building that looks like it's made of cinder blocks. A red-faced young man wearing a rain-spattered jacket comes out of it as soon as I drive up to the pumps. His face is shaped like a bell, wider at the bottom than the top. A spray of pimples makes a half-circle around the right side of his mouth.

I ask him if he has a map of the county. He nods, smirking, as if he sees some sort of private irony in the request. He comes back a few minutes later, holding a map in one hand.

"Dollar and a quarter," he says.

I pay him and spread the map on the passenger seat to look for the streets I didn't recognize last night. A knock on the window makes me look up. The young man is leaning his fists on the driver's side door, frowning. I roll down the window.

"You trying to get somewheres special?" he asks.

"Actually, there's a couple of streets I can't find. I don't seem to be able—"

" 'Preciate it you could keep this area here clear for the other customers."

I glance in the rearview mirror. The road is empty.

"Okay," I say. "Thanks for the map."

He steps away, leaning back against one of the pumps. He's still there when I look in the rearview mirror again a few yards down the road.

The first address on my list turns out to be a trailer court. There's a gravel road, and the numbers are nailed to the sides of each trailer. The one I want doesn't look vastly different from the rest. It's white, and tracks of rust run down the window sills and around the door. The front stoop is a plastic milk crate, and I don't have to test it to see whether it'll bear my weight. Instead, I reach up and knock on the door, which is a good two feet off the ground.

A young woman answers; a girl, really. Her hair is bleached almost white and she has on a nightgown with a sweatshirt over it. A child clings to her legs, a dirty-faced little boy who stares at me with big blue eyes. I guess he is not more than two years old.

"I'm sorry to bother you," I say. "I'm looking for Reis Paley."

"Who wants him?"

"I'm an old friend of his. I moved away a while back and I was trying to get in touch with him again, but—"

The girl cuts me off. "Nobody here by that name."

"Then why did you want to know who was looking for him?"

She shrugs. "Bored, I guess." She looks past me at the backdrop of fog, wet trees, patchy ground. "Thought you was maybe selling them encyclopedias. They don't usually come around till the summer."

"Is your name Paley?"

"Na."

"Is there anyone living here by that name?"

"Na."

My hair falls wet across my eyes. I pushed it away, and tap my foot on the milk crate. "I don't understand. The phone book listed someone named Paley living at this address."

"Oh, I don't live here," the girl replies. "I just be renting." Just then, the child tugs at her nightgown and she looks down at him. "For Pete's *sake* Schuyler," she says irritably, "can't you see I'm having an adult conversation here?"

The child moans.

I ask the girl if she'd mind telling me how I could get in touch with the person she rents from.

She blows through her lips. "Shoo, I don't know," she says. "My husband pays the bills."

"May I speak to him then?"

"Na, he's to work."

"When will he be home?"

She draws back, suddenly suspicious. "Soon. Real soon."

For an instant, I see myself through her eyes: a strange man, wet and red-faced, eyes tearing, a desperate look on his face.

"Here's my card," I tell her, pulling out my wallet and handing one up to her. "I'd appreciate it if your husband would give me call when he gets home."

She studies it. "I don't think he's going to call no long distance to New York."

"Right. Sorry. Do you have a pen? I have a local number."

"More'n likely."

She and the child disappear inside the trailer, and I hear her pushing things around. I stamp my feet to keep warm. A few minutes later, she comes back holding a pencil stub, and writes down the number I give her. She reads it over and looks at me.

"Okay," she says.

"You'll remember to tell your husband, won't you?"

She tilts her head and raises one fine eyebrow. "Well gosh, maybe, if I remember to strap my brain in."

"I'm sorry. It's just that it's very important."

"Sure, I get it. Old friend."

"No, honestly. We had a sort of falling out just before I moved away, and now I want to tell him I was wrong about something."

Why, I wonder, am I telling this to a complete stranger? Is the need for absolution so strong? Or is it simply unspecific: if the offended party isn't available, any substitute willing to listen will suffice?

"Huh." The girl plucks a piece of lint off her sweatshirt and lets it flutter to the ground.

"So I would appreciate it very much if your husband would give me a call."

The child reappears and grips his mother's leg, making her flinch. "*Godammit Schuyler,*" she snaps. "You get away from this door before you catch pneumonia and die. Is that what you want? You want Mommy to spend the rest of her life crying because you're too stubborn to do what she tells you once in a while?"

The child looks up at her, blinking, and then starts to bawl. The girl swoops down to pick him up, heaving a groan as she stands again. The child presses his face in her neck while she pats him on the back and coos in his ear. She looks down at me.

"I gotta get him inside. He's a handful, as you can probably guess."

"He's a beautiful boy," I tell her. "I'm sure he'll turn out all right. Thank you for your time."

She smiles, a grateful mother, and as I turn around heading back to my car, she calls after me. I turn back. She's standing at the half-closed door, jiggling the child up and down in her arms.

"Good luck," she says. "I mean—good luck."

It takes almost an hour to find the second address. By then the rain has stopped, and a pallid sun has broken through the clouds. The second place is a two-story red house with spruce trees pressing against either side. For a good five minutes, I stand shivering on the porch, alternately knocking and ringing the bell.

No one comes to the door.

Back at my grandmother's, I place a call into my answering service, but there aren't any messages. So much for being missed. The receptionist at Richard's office—my next call—informs me that he's at the hospital. When I try him there, however, he doesn't answer his page. Finally, I phone our apartment, and listen to my voice on the outgoing message, cheerily telling callers I'll be out of town for a couple of weeks.

In the parlor, the empty cardboard boxes lined up against the wall seem to accuse me of neglect. So, with a brief sigh of self-pity and resignation, I decide to start with the linen closet, nearly gagging from the smell of mothballs when I open the door. I push my arm in as far as I can reach, and sweep an entire shelf of pills, bottles, ointments, bandages, cotton balls, cotton swabs, and denture creams onto the floor. I move to the next higher shelf and send a pile of towels and wash cloths tumbling. The sheets next. Hat boxes. A sewing kit. Clothes that have never been worn, still wrapped in tissue paper that flutters open and closed at my feet, like wings.

By dinnertime, I've managed to fill every one of the boxes I'd collected from the Dumpster the night before. It doesn't seem like I've made much progress, though. I wasted the first couple of hours, handling things, smelling them, hoping maybe to uncover a clue—a missing piece, which, when snapped into place, will fill the empty part of the life puzzle that won't stay still, but insists on moving restlessly around, making mischief in my head.

I don't feel filled, though.
Full, but not filled.

A few days after Neal Armstrong walked on the moon, I took Reis to the quarry as a way of making up for prying about his father. The quarry was a secret place, about three miles south of my grandmother's house. It was set on the top of a steep hill, surrounded by dense woods. You had to be born in Amity to know about it, and not even all the locals were aware of its existence.

When my father had brought me there for the first time, he made me promise two things: first, to preserve what he called a long and honorable tradition of secrecy; and second, never to go there alone. I wasn't sure if I was breaking my first promise by taking Reis to the quarry. But even if he wasn't born in Amity, he was living there, and I had a good idea he could keep a secret better than most.

We could only ride our bicycles a few hundred yards up the trail—there were too many trees after that—so we left them hidden behind some bushes and headed up the rest of the way on foot. Not even halfway to the top, we were already sweating hard. My legs and arms itched as if they'd been bitten by a swarm of mosquitoes.

Suddenly, a woodpecker shot up into the air. I turned to watch it go, its red crest incandescent against the darker foliage; and because I wasn't watching where I was going, I tripped on a tree root and somersaulted nearly perfectly, scraping a patch of skin off my leg above the knee. When I came limping out of the woods, Reis was already sitting on the edge of the quarry, looking down at the water thirty feet below. I sat down next to him.

"Thinking of jumping?" I asked.

"Na. Maybe falling. You're cut."

"Yeah."

"We can't have anything nice, can we?" Reis said, imitating his mother's tone. He brought out a wrinkled pack of cigarettes from his pants pocket and handed one across to me.

"I never smoked before," I confessed.

"Ain't nothin'." Reis lit a match and touched the flame to the end of each of our cigarettes. "Pull in a good breath and let it go."

He watched me closely.

"How's that feel then?"

"Dizzy."

"That'll pass."

"Where'd you get these anyhow?"

"I have my ways."

"Your mom."

"Ain't her brand, are they, sharp eyes?"

His mother smoked True Blues; these were Lucky Strikes.

"You didn't get these from Oleg down to the package store," I said, more a question than a statement. "He hates kids."

Reis didn't think it worth any comment.

"He's crazy, that Oleg," I added.

"He don't hate kids. Least not all kids."

"Can't tell me you got these from him."

Reis blew smoke out the corner of his mouth, and squinted at me. "Why's that?"

"You stole them."

"I said I got my ways."

"It's a sin."

He shrugged. "If you believe in it, I guess it is."

"You're not afraid of hell?"

"Don't know nobody come back yet to tell of it."

To me, the rules had always been clear. Good people obeyed the Ten Commandments, took communion, and tried to act like Jesus;

when they died, they were rewarded in heaven. Bad people didn't do any of these things, not because they didn't know any better, but because they didn't want to. And when they died, they suffered in hell.

I knew there were other types of Christians, but they had their own rules.

I asked Reis if he was a Protestant.

He blew an impressively controlled stream of smoke.

"We used to go to the Holy Rollers, but only to make my dad's family happy. My mom says we're going to be Catholic up here. Gonna go to Catholic school and all that. Cut yourself pretty good," he said, changing the subject.

He pressed his thumb over the gash.

"That hurt?"

I shook my head no and he applied more pressure, till blood oozed out past his thumb.

"How about that?"

"Nope."

He drew a bloody line up and down my leg. "Bet it will."

He pressed his thumb just under the cuff of my shorts so hard I flinched and jerked my leg away. Immediately, he turned his attention back to his cigarette, taking one last puff and crushing the burning end on the rock rim. He tossed it out over the water and I followed his example, but the water was so far down we could barely hear when they hit.

The air sang with crickets and a white haze blurred the trees on the other side of the quarry.

"You ready to go in?" Reis asked.

We kicked off our sneakers and tossed them behind us, along with our T-shirts and shorts. My bathing suit had come in a bag with a lot of other hand-me-downs from a second cousin of my mother's I didn't even know; it was baggy, and hung practically to my knees. I should have just kept my shorts on, but it was too late now. Reis was staring.

"It's pretty dumb, isn't it?" I said.

"Take it off, then."

I looked around, as if someone might have heard. "Sure," I replied, sarcastically.

"Don't tell me you ain't been skinny-dippin' ever?"

I looked at him blankly.

"Judas Priest," he said. "You got a sheltered life, little brother."

Abruptly, he pulled down his bathing suit and kicked it on top of the pile of our other things. I hadn't seen another boy naked since I was four years old, the last time Mrs. Hewitt put Toby and me in the same tub. I had no idea what the rules were now, at thirteen, or what to do with the terrible self-consciousness.

Reis came over and tugged at the waistband of my suit. "Well come on, then."

"Quit it," I shouted, my voice breaking. I shoved his hand away.

"Suit yourself."

Reis walked away to the edge of the cliff. Now that he was no longer facing me, I could look at him, at his body, which seemed so much stronger than mine. By comparison, I looked like a skeleton. He raised his hands over his head and, arcing out over the rim, disappeared. I heard his voice, wailing like some sort of ecstatic bird, and then the sound of his body hitting the water.

I stood where I was, listening to him splash around thirty feet below. Then I walked to the edge and jumped. As always, a sick feeling seized me in mid-fall: I was suddenly sure the water would drain away completely before I landed, and I'd be smashed against dry rock. Or a giant creature would be waiting in the deep, tentacles poised to drag me down. Then I hit the water, and after the first shock of cold exhilaration pumped through me, my heart started racing and my arms and legs thrashed.

Usually, this exhilaration lasted till I was exhausted, but today it faded much sooner. I was jealous, watching Reis glide so effortlessly through the water. I struggled to keep up with him, constantly adjusting my suit, which clung heavily around my legs. I wished I could swim naked, but it was too late. One of the most important rules of being a boy was that, once you made a choice, you had to defend it with your life.

After taking a shower, I call Richard. He groans when I ask him where he's been all day.

"Day from hell," he says. "It started with Davis—the one you call the exotic dancer—calling to say he had some sort of scabs on his leg. They weren't scabs, it was a staph infection. Half his leg was gone. He put *Vaseline* on it, hoping it would go away, said he didn't think it was serious. I mean, what does it take?"

"Sometimes a staph infection."

"I told him with his cell count, a pimple is serious."

"Bully for you."

"That was for starters. After that there were about a hundred cases of strep, and twice that number of flus. And one hysteric with a brown spot on his arm he thought was a sarcoma. It was a contusion. Ugly, but basically a boo-boo."

"Richard, you didn't say boo-boo, did you?"

"I did not. I merely suggested that if he cut back his drinking, he might not fall down as much. Which is, in many cases, the pathogeny of boo-boos."

Richard's explanation jars something I've managed, perhaps conveniently, to forget after twenty-odd years. Slowly, as if through a process of inverse regeneration, the bruises on my mother's arms and legs become visible once again, reasserting themselves in memory with nearly the same gradual yet inevitable intensity with which they'd appeared in the flesh.

I'd begun to notice these bruises sometime during the year after my father's death. They looked fairly ordinary at first; the natural, if unpleasant, consequence of passing out on a regular basis. I didn't discuss them with either my mother or my grandmother—and the very idea of mentioning them to anyone outside the immediate family never even occurred to me.

This initially didn't bother me as much as the failure to respond later on, when the bruises began to grow more livid, and her lips began to chap and bleed. She became paler and quieter every week, while the tumors grew—in her liver, in her breast, in her lungs—and a kind of household martial law effectively forbade discussion of all unhappy topics. As though with my father's death we'd all reached a saturation point—a tacit understanding that in a contest between unpleasantness and death, death was the clear favorite.

I simply didn't connect the woman slowly rotting in the bedroom down the hall with the one who had taught me how to dance only a few years earlier. Only one of them had been my mother. The other one didn't have a name.

"How was your day?" Richard asks. "Find any buried treasure in the old house?"

"Not yet. I'm still looking."

"Good. I want to retire."

"No, you don't."

"No, I guess not."

I can tell by the sound of his voice that he's winding down now. Or maybe he doesn't want to overdo it, remembering the last time he'd made up too many stories to account for the time he'd been spending in someone else's bed.

The last time, I was home waiting for him; past midnight some nights, until I gave up and turned out the lights. At some point I'd wake to the sound of the shower running, and for a couple of seconds I'd be afraid it was morning already and I'd overslept my alarm. But the room was dark, and the clock by the bed read 2:00 or 3:00 A.M., and I'd turn on my stomach and fall back to sleep until Richard finally climbed into bed, still damp from his shower, and turn on his side, away from me.

"I think I'll heat up the rest of the lasagna in the freezer and go to bed," he says now.

"Cheese before sleep gives you bad dreams."

"Really? Did Freud say that?"

"No. Grandma Fowler."

"Sounds like a smart lady."

"She was," I reply. Then, after a couple of seconds, I tell him I'm sorry.

"For what?" he asks, surprised.

"For being a disappointing lover. Distant. Self-centered."

He's silent a moment, measuring his response.

"Your grandmother's dead," he says, "and you're probably experiencing some sort of remorse."

"I don't think so, Richard. I think this has more to do with simply telling you I'm sorry."

"Aha." He exhales noisily. "I don't know what to do with that."

"Nothing. Maybe there's nothing to do."

"Then why say anything at all?" Anger creeps into his tone now. "You're God knows how far away, it's ten o'clock at night, and out of the blue you say you're sorry—and then nothing, don't eat the lasagna, it'll give you bad dreams?"

"You're probably right. I'm reacting to my grandmother's death."

"Well," he replies, mollified.

"Yes."

"Alright."

We toss a few more nonsense words back and forth until it's alright to hang up. Afterward, I stand holding onto the receiver and listening to the dial tone, marveling at both the effort involved in not seeing certain types of bruises and the disturbing passions that come to the surface when blindness is suddenly, cruelly, cured.

At the end of the summer, Reis came down sick. It was hardly more than a summer cold, his mother insisted, so my grandmother told me it was all right to visit him.

When I rang the front doorbell, he came to the door in just his pajama bottoms, his hair mussed and dirty.

"Come on in," he said. "My mom's to work. You want something to drink?"

"If you're going to."

"You don't got to be so polite for Christ's sake."

We went to the kitchen, where Reis poured us each a glass of lemonade from a pitcher in the refrigerator.

"My mom made it special for me this morning," he said. "But I figured out how to go it one better."

"What's that?"

"Just wait and see, little brother."

He dragged a chair from the kitchen table over to a tall cupboard. Climbing onto the chair, he opened the topmost door, and extracted a bottle of Seagram's whiskey from the cupboard. Then he climbed back down from the chair, and poured an inch or so in each of our glasses, squinting like a Wild West bartender.

"Here's mud in your eye," he said.

I'd never really had much experience with alcohol, outside a sip or two of my father's beer or my mother's highball when I was little. This glaring deficiency in my education had no moral or logical basis in my mother's condition. It was not only possible to live with a drunk mother without using her drinking to predict the possible results of one's own experiments—it was, in a sense, a profoundly necessary disassociation. When I heard my mother vomiting in the bathroom, for example, or found myself ambushed by the sickly stink of alcohol and body odor that sometimes escaped her bedroom, I was able to separate these impressions into their own mental compartment. I never really had to think about detaching in this way; the process occurred more or less automatically.

Except when she tried to talk to me.

Every once in a while she'd wait just inside her bedroom door, catching me as I came galloping down the stairs on my way out to meet Reis somewhere.

"Where're you going now?" she'd demand, slurring the words without managing to obscure the hurt behind them.

"Out," I'd reply.

"Out. Always running out."

"It's a nice day out."

Sometimes she'd advance a step or two, careful to keep one hand on the doorknob. With the other, she might reach out and touch my face.

"Remember we used to play Chinese checkers together?" she might ask. "Didn't we have fun?"

I'd remember, but pretend not to. It was too easy, otherwise, to get stuck listening to other things she wanted to remember. Which usually ended up with her crying, wrapping her thin arms around my shoulders and shaking while she cursed God for all the evils that had befallen her, chief among which were convincing her to marry a man who didn't love her and then taking him away. She was, of course, blind to the paradox of that complaint.

With practice, I learned to sidle down the hall step by awkward step until I was far enough away to say I had to go, that I was running late, I had to meet someone.

"Some girl, some little flirt," she'd shout after me.

That particular accusation made it all the harder to see any parallel between my mother's pathetic behavior and my standing in Reis's kitchen trying on a glass of spiked lemonade for size.

I took a cautious sip. Although the smell stung a bit more sharply than I'd expected, the taste wasn't altogether unpleasant. I took another quick swallow while Reis drained his own glass and poured more whiskey in it. He told me to finish up, and after I obliged he poured an inch more in my glass. Then he carried the bottle to the sink and ran a thin stream of tap water into it.

"What's that for?"

Reis looked at me as if I'd suddenly gone simple.

"So she won't see if there's any missing."

He replaced the bottle, and dragged the chair back to the kitchen table. Then he picked up his glass, and held it out to me.

"Cheers."

"Like this?" I asked. "No lemonade?"

"Christ Mary, little brother. You got to learn to drink it straight. You walk into a bar someday and order a whiskey and lemonade, they'll laugh you out the door."

I took long swallow and immediately set the glass down. Sweat sprang across my forehead and my eyes momentarily went all fuzzy. I said I thought I'd hold on for a little while.

"Sure," he replied. "No sense throwing it all back up on the kitchen floor. Stay right here. I'll be right back."

He ran out of the room while I sat at the kitchen table. After a few more sips, the whiskey started to work on me. The kitchen started to look brighter. I was happy just to be sitting there, staring out into the backyard: at the poplars turning silver leaf-backs in the wind, the rose beds and purple azaleas Mrs. Paley fussed over. I drifted into a sort of daydream, imagining Reis and me living in the house by ourselves, staying up as late as we wanted, making frozen dinners, and drinking whiskey and lemonade.

After a while, Reis padded back into the kitchen carrying a pile of comic books and a pack of cigarettes on top of it. An unlit one dangled from his mouth. He dumped the comic books on the table in front of me, then went to the counter for an ashtray and matches. When he returned to the table, he lit his cigarette, and passed one to me. I asked him if it didn't hurt his throat to smoke.

He replied that a person had to learn to be tough.

Reis tossed the burnt match into the ashtray, then pushed his chair closer to me and opened a comic book between us. We read about a witch who came back every hundred years to take revenge on the descendants of the judge who'd had her burned at the stake; then one about a magician, who hypnotized people to make them carry out crimes on his behalf.

Reis asked me if I'd ever been hypnotized, but before I could answer, I got the hiccups.

"What're you, drunk?" he asked.

"Just the hiccups."

"Well you know what the best cure is don't you?"

"Swallow a spoonful of sugar."

Reis shook his head. "That don't work. But I know what does."

He stood up from the table and crossed to the counter. After digging a while through a small bowl full of junk, he came back with a necklace that had a sort of disk strung on it, studded with rhinestones.

"The close is broke," he said. "She keeps meaning to bring it to a store to get it fixed but she doesn't. Typical."

He dangled the necklace in front of my face and told me to relax. I actually did try. It was hard going at first, to stifle my hiccups; but after a couple of minutes they stopped on their own. When I closed my eyes, I could feel Reis's breath warm on my face, the smell of liquor on it, and something else. Salty, spicy.

He told me to raise my right arm, just like the comic book magician had told his victims to test his power over them. Then Reis ordered me to open my eyes and go to the sink, fill a glass with water, and drink it down in one gulp. Which I did, pretending to be in a trance, thinking it was only a game.

Next, he told me to come back to the table. I walked back slowly, staring straight ahead, the way I imagined someone sleepwalking would do it. Reis commanded me to get down on my knees, and then to repeat after him that I was his servant and would obey his every command.

Unfortunately, in the middle of my recitation the hiccups made an abrupt and spectacular return. I could feel my face turn red.

"Had you going there for a while, didn't I?" I said, once the fit had passed.

Reis stared at me for almost a full minute.

"Sure," he replied finally. Then he got up from his chair. "I'm kind of tired now. Maybe you better go on."

I left, promising to return the next day.

When I showed up the following afternoon, though, he wouldn't answer the door. I went around to the backyard and threw a couple of stones at Reis's bedroom window, but the only response was the angry chattering of birds nesting nearby. So I went back to the front yard and stood a while looking up and down the road: at the trees grown suddenly immense, the sky impossibly distant. For the first time that summer, I didn't know what to do with myself. Eventually, I got back on my bicycle and rode back up the hill toward my grandmother's house.

There was a stickball game going on in the field outside the old barn. I'd raced by on my way to see Reis, but now I stopped and hoisted my bike over the fence and leaned against the rails to watch. Dana shouted over for me to join them, which I did.

I was surprised by how much I enjoyed playing with my old friends again. I felt as if I'd just come out of a long sleep full of anxious dreams. After the game, I sat with Dana and Toby and some of the other boys in the shade of the barn, leaning our backs against the wood. Dana stretched his legs out and observed that I was spending a lot of time with the Paley kid.

To which I replied, shrugging it off, that it was only because my grandmother told me I ought to be friendly.

"You better watch out," Dana warned.

"Why's that?"

"I asked him to come over and play some pool in the cellar when he first moved in. And while we were down there he started acting goofy."

"Goofy how?"

"*Goofy.* You know." Dana looked past me at Toby. "Hey, do how he goes down the street."

Toby stood up and imitated the way Reis walked, slowly and deliberately, swiveling his hips, which made everybody laugh. When he sat down again, Charlie Holubeck told us that only the day before he'd overheard his mother telling one of her girlfriends that the Paleys hadn't left Alabama exactly by choice. But when his mother had seen him listening at the door, she and her friend immediately changed the subject and started talking instead about a sale on ground beef at Beuckman's grocery store.

As I rode down the hill toward home, I tried to decipher precisely what Dana might have meant by *goofy*. No doubt, I made the process more complicated by ignoring the explanations that sprang immediately to mind. It wasn't that they were impossible to believe; I had every reason to believe them.

But this meant that I had every reason to believe that I might end up being called goofy, too.

Accordingly, I went on my own to church the following Saturday afternoon. My shoes seemed to make a thunderous noise, clicking on the gray stone tiles the lined the aisle. The powdery scent of myrrh filled my nostrils. The cool air inside the church enfolded me, and the light in the sanctuary seemed to have a dim, amniotic quality. It shimmered with pockets of richer color where candles burned in blue jars at the feet of a plaster Virgin and red jars beneath Jesus on the cross. I could almost have been swimming.

Quickly genuflecting, I slid into an empty pew near the front of the church. The wood rubbed by countless bodies felt smooth and comforting as skin. Two other people waited their turn ahead of me: an old woman with orange hair I recognized from town and a man I'd never seen before. The woman rocked back and forth in her pew, her eyes locked on the face of the Virgin, a rosary clicking softly through her fingers as she told it. I could see only the man's profile, the long nose and caved cheeks of his bowed head.

I folded my hands on the back of the pew in front of me and shut my eyes for a while. When I opened them again, the woman was gone and only the man remained, so still he might have been carved from wax. Even after the orange-haired woman came out of the confessional, he continued to sit that way, oblivious to her steps echoing on the stone floor, and the groan she let out as she knelt in front of the Virgin's statue. I waited until I was sure he wasn't going anywhere before making my way to the confessional.

The wooden door clicked shut behind me. I knelt in the darkness, holding my breath for a second because the woman before me had left behind a strong scent of perfume. After a while, came the faint hiss of a panel being slid across the small square opening; my signal to begin.

"Forgive me father," I whispered, "for I have sinned."

"How have you sinned?" he replied.

Father Wood had been a part of my life ever since I could remember. The rounds he made through the parish brought him to my grandmother's at least once a month.

"My son?" he pressed.

"Thoughts," I replied quickly. "Sinful thoughts."

After a few moments, he coughed.

"Proceed."

I didn't answer, preoccupied with trying to feel the floor under my knees and the thin wall between the priest and me. I was there, and then I wasn't anymore.

Only the sound of my footsteps as I ran back down the aisle proved my existence, swallowing the shouts of the old priest leaning out from the confessional, the startled look of the woman turning from her unfinished prayer, and the serenely indifferent figure of a man I'd never seen before sleeping in an otherwise empty pew.

Ashes

I did not see Reis again until two weeks after Dana warned me about spending time alone with him.

The first day of school had arrived and my childhood friends and I were entering seventh grade. Although the seventh grade classes would meet in the familiar Mother of Sorrows School building, the move upward into junior high school figured as a significant transition. At our sixth-grade graduation ceremony, the various teachers who spoke impressed upon us that we were leaving childhood things behind, and could now look forward to taking on new, more adult responsibilities.

Not surprisingly, I dawdled by the kitchen window for a long time. Dana and Toby would only wait a minute or two in front of their own houses, then they would head up to school together, according to a long-standing arrangement among the three of us: Whoever wasn't outside in the morning had either gone on ahead already or was sick in bed.

My grandmother came out of her bedroom closing the last button of the smock she wore at the five and dime.

"Going be late," she said, glancing at the clock.

I told her I wasn't feeling very well.

She came over and put her hand on my forehead. "Don't got fever," she announced. "You trying to get out the first day school?"

"I really don't feel good."

She smiled. "You ain't the first boy I raised, I know all the tricks." She opened the refrigerator and pulled out a paper sack. "Take your lunch now and get. Here. Take a dime for your milk money."

I crossed to the table and put my lunch in my book bag. When I turned around, my grandmother was smiling, hiding one hand in the big front pocket of her smock.

"Got something for you to the store yesterday," she said, and pulled out a chocolate bar. "Can't have you go the first day school looking like a poor boy."

I didn't make a move to take it.

"What's a matter?" she asked, frowning. "You afraid of something to school?"

"Na."

I took the candy bar and gave her a kiss her on the cheek. She tipped her head back, the better to see me.

"Getting so big," she observed, sadly. "Soon you'll be growed up and leave poor Grandma all alone."

"Nu-uh," I replied, and she kissed me again, actually covering my face with kisses the way she'd done when I was small and could sit on her lap.

I dawdled up the hill and down the other side. When I came to the fork in the road, I was tempted not to turn at all, but just head on straight to school. But my grandmother had already promised Roberta Paley that I'd walk with Reis, so he wouldn't have to go alone on the first day of school.

I stood waiting next to the rose of Sharon tree in the front yard, hoping he wouldn't see me so I'd have an excuse for not going to school with him. Reis came out of the house, though, and we started down the road side by side. I asked him how his sore throat was, and he replied that it was better. After that, we didn't have anything more to say to each other.

We took a shortcut through the meadow, and then turned north back onto the road when we saw the school. Cars were pulling in and out of the lot to let off groups of two and three kids at a time. A crossing guard wearing a bright orange belt around her chest and waist directed the stream of traffic, and walked groups of children from one side of the street to the other. Squealing and shouting tore the air.

I hurried ahead of Reis into the schoolyard, relieved to have done my duty and put an end to it. My friends had gathered in the soccer field. I headed toward them, but the bell rang before I reached them, so I turned back and joined the crowd of students filing into the school.

The seventh-grade classroom smelled of fresh paint. The blinds had been pulled up precisely to the same height, forming a seamless line of white across the windows. Seating in all Mother of Sorrows classrooms had always been assigned alphabetically, so I went immediately to my place next to a boy named Casper Frenz, beside whom I'd sat every year since first grade. At lunchtime, I managed to wedge myself between Dana and Toby, leaving Reis to eat by himself on the other side of the cafeteria.

I couldn't escape quite so easily at the end of the day, though. Reis stood waiting for me at the front door of the school. I told him I had to go to the bathroom, and for a minute I was afraid he'd want to come with me. But he merely nodded and told me he'd meet me on the front steps.

I hurried down the hall to the boys' bathroom and counted to a hundred before quietly pushing open the heavy wooden swinging door to reconnoiter. To my great relief, I didn't see Reis anywhere in the hall.

Creeping cautiously, I made my way to the back door of the school building and out through the faculty parking lot. While my heart thumped with what felt like an exceedingly loud, irregular rhythm, I climbed the fence between the school and the house next door, crossed the street, then jogged over the hill into the meadow, fairly galloping through the tall yellow grass. Almost immediately, a cramp seized my calf; but I was too worried about putting enough distance between myself and the school to stop. By the time I noticed the group of older boys sitting under a tree it was already too late to turn around.

There were three of them, all with long hair and sparse goatees. In spite of the afternoon heat and humidity, they all had on heavy-looking black leather jackets.

They looked up when they heard me running down the path. I recognized one of them by the scar under his eye. His name was Kyle Gorman. I'd known him as a delinquent since he was eight years old, when my mother pointed him out in the Beuckman's back lot, smoking with boys twice his age.

"Hey punk," he called now.

I set my face and split off the dirt trail into the grass. Unfortunately, between the cramp in my leg and the exhaustion of running, I couldn't move fast enough to keep Kyle from heading me off.

"What's the matter, you don't hear?" he asked, standing in front of me with his hands on his hips.

He was easily a foot taller than I. Up close, the scar under his eye looked like a bolt of lightning.

"I heard you," I replied breathlessly.

"So why didn't you answer?"

The two boys he'd been sitting with now made their way over, flanking me on all sides.

"Maybe he's a idiot," one of them said.

Kyle studied me solemnly. "Are you a idiot?"

I shook my head no.

The third boy pressed a cigarette between his lips and lit it. "If he was," he muttered, "how the hell would he know?"

"What's your name?" Kyle asked me.

"Christian."

They seemed to think that was funny, nodding at each other and prodding each other with their elbows.

"It's Chris," I amended.

Kyle raised an eyebrow. "Which is it?"

The one with the cigarette stepped behind me now and yanked my collar.

"Maybe he got it pinned inside his shirt."

He wrenched my collar around.

"Nope," he said. "Just says Sears. Maybe his name's Sears."

They thought this was funny, too.

"Look, his face is turning red," the second boy announced.

"You're choking him, Brian," Kyle said. "Let go his collar."

"Maybe it's the sun. Maybe he's getting sunburn. What color is it now?"

"Purple."

"Let go his collar, Brian."

Kyle stepped in closer, grabbed my book bag, and turned it upside down, shaking it till the books tumbled out on the grass. He picked one up and opened it, reading aloud from the list of names at the front until he came to the last name on the list.

"Buddy Hill," he read, then looked up at me. "That your name then? Buddy?"

I shook my no, but I was too scared to explain that I hadn't had time to write my own name at the bottom of the list. Sweat had begun to run down my face, and collect in itchy pockets under my shirt.

"Tell you what, Buddy," Kyle said. "You can be our buddy. How would you like that?"

"Fine," I replied.

"Fine." Kyle grinned at the other two boys. "He said fine." He looked back at me. "Well that's just dandy, Buddy. There's one thing I forgot to mention, the initiation. It ain't much, though, nothin' a be scared of."

He showed me his hand. There was a roughly circular pink scar, about a quarter of an inch wide, across on the palm.

"We all got one, see," he said. "The mark of Zero."

The boy holding my collar gave it another twist, and wrapped his free arm around my waist. I became acutely conscious of the noise of grasshoppers and bees, and could almost feel the sky's weight bending the grass and drooping the leaves of trees all around me. I tried to keep from shaking as Kyle stepped closer and grabbed my hand and flattened it. The second boy lit a cigarette, and brought the lit end toward my palm. After that, I couldn't hear anything else but the sound of my own screaming.

I saw Reis's shadow first, while I was kneeling by the creek, cooling my hand in the water. He sat down next to me and examined my hand.

"Christ Mary," he said. "You should of waited on me."

I shook my head, confused.

"Or I should of waited on you," he continued. "Except I got so damn thirsty waiting out on that school porch, I thought there'd have to be a place somewhere to get a Coke." He scooped some water in his palm and let it dribble onto the burn. "They'd of never done this if there'd been two of us."

"Maybe."

"Damn. I should of waited on you."

I was sure he was lying. But it seemed to be a different kind of lie than I was familiar with. It had nothing to do with covering his tracks, or protecting himself, or getting out of doing something he didn't want to do. Nothing to do with deceiving me, even; as if lying was the best way to tell me he knew I'd purposely abandoned him, and why, and that whatever had come between us before was now finished.

"We'll fix you up at my house," he said.

"I better just go home."

"And what? Give your poor old grandma a stroke and have her worry every time you leave the house? Christ Mary, use some sense little brother."

"Quit that. You're not any older than me."

Without asking my permission, he simply picked up my book bag along with his own, and started walking up the bank and across the meadow.

A few seconds later, I stood up and followed.

"What sort of things you got to fix this up with?" I asked.

"Iodine. Band-Aids. The usual stuff."

"What'll I say about being bandaged?"

"Say you fell. Say we was playing stickball."

"She'll know it's a fib."

Reis looked at me sideways. "Say it was tag then. Say we was horsing around." He shoved his shoulder into me.

"Hey."

"Ain't such a fib now. I knocked into you."

As we climbed out of the meadow, a flock of birds flew from the trees, printing points of darkness against the milk-blue sky. We made our way east down the road; and when cars came by, we went single file, waving our hands in front of our faces to ward off the dust and dry leaves that trailed in their wake.

Reis let us inside with a key strung on a rabbit's foot. I followed him into the kitchen first, where he poured us each a glass of orange

Kool-Aid. Afterward, we headed upstairs to the bathroom. I sat on the toilet lid while Reis cleaned and bandaged my hand; the iodine stung and the bandage felt thick and clumsy on my palm.

When he was finished fixing me up, we went down the hall to his room. Inside, Reis peeled off his shirt and threw it in a corner. His chest was bigger than mine, and tufts of blond hair showed under his arms.

"Hot up here," he murmured. "Make yourself at home."

The room was small, cluttered with model airplanes, stacks of comic books, and dirty clothes. Over the bed, hung a poster of the *Apollo* spaceship.

"You want to be an astronaut?" I asked.

"My mom thinks so," Reis replied. "I let her go on believing." He flopped belly down on his bed and grabbed some comic books off the nearest stack. "What do you want to read?"

I stood in the middle of the room, shifting from foot to foot. "How come you and your mom moved up here?"

Reis's expression didn't change. "We neither one of us could like it very much down there."

"Charlie Holubeck said his mother said you *had* to move up here."

"You believe everything you hear?"

"Not everything."

We stayed looking at each other, until finally Reis rolled over on his back and put his arms under his head and gazed up at the ceiling.

"It's like this," he said. "There was a kid a couple of years younger than me, and we were out swimming together one day and he drowned. That's all."

"That's why you moved?"

"That's it, little brother."

"Was he a friend of yours?"

"Sometime."

"He was younger than you?"

"Two, three year."

"What was his name?"

"What's it got to do with anything?"

"Nothing."

"Lee McKibben. That enough for you, Curious George?"

"Guess so."

Neither of us said anything for a minute.

"I only didn't tell you because I thought you wouldn't be my friend. Seems like you're the only around here worth being friends with anyhow. Everyone else's duller than a sack a hammers."

"They aren't so bad when you get to know them."

"Skunk's a skunk even when you catch its smell."

"Well."

"So you still my friend?" Reis asked.

The question sounded small and far away.

"You bet," I replied.

My voice cracked as I said this.

Something else cracked, too. It felt like a wall of thin glass wrapped around an emptiness inside, which could either harden or break, the choice was mine. And knowing even this much scared me in a way that nothing had before. I flattened myself on the bed next to Reis, and told him not to be a dope.

Reis lay quite still a few seconds longer. Abruptly, he flipped over and put his arms around my waist and squeezed. We both pulled away almost immediately.

For the next half hour, we lay beside each other on the bed reading comic books, our feet knocking against each other from time to time, elbows touching. Afternoon shadows grew dense around us, and when I eventually looked at the clock, it read half past five.

I sat up quickly. "I'd better be going."

"You still got that medal I give you?"

"You want it back?"

"Na. Besides, she'd know something if it suddenly turned up again."

"That's true."

Suddenly, he grinned. "You ever get me mad I'll tell her I saw you steal it."

"Says you," I replied, heading for the door. "I'll tell her the truth."

"Either way you got something don't belong to you, little brother."

"I told you to quit that."

"I'm just teasing." Reis jumped off the bed and bounded across the room to block the door. "Make two fists with your hands."

"What for?"

"Just do it for Christ's sake."

He grabbed my wrists and pulled them so that my fists connected with his face: one-two, a light slow-motion punch.

"Oh that's bad," he pronounced, shaking his head. "Very bad. You can't defend yourself."

"So who cares?"

I pushed past him out the door.

It was cooler downstairs, but as soon as I stepped outside, heat and humidity collapsed around me like a wet towel. Reis followed me to the front door and pressed himself against the screen, fingering the aluminum scroll work on the inside. Behind him, the interior of the house looked completely dark.

"Soon as that hand heals up I can teach you how to box," he said. "I'm not too bad at it. Want to give it a try?"

I thought it over a moment. "Maybe. That way you ever get *me* mad I could whomp you."

I stepped off the porch.

"What're you going to tell your grandma about your hand?"

"Like you said. I fell."

I turned around and headed across the front yard.

"Don't go taking them Band-Aids off for a couple of days, hear?" Reis shouted after me. "Not even if you take a bath."

My grandmother was pulling up in her car just as I reached her house. She smiled and waved when she saw me come down the hill.

"Where you coming from?" she asked.

"I went to Reis's after school."

"What you got on your hand?"

"Band-Aid. We were horsing around and I fell. Doesn't hurt much."

"Good. Then you can help bring these groceries inside."

I took two of the bags, leaving the lightest one for her to carry. While she changed out of her work clothes, I unloaded all three bags into the pantry and refrigerator.

"You had good day to school?" she asked, when she came out of her room again.

"Okay." I hefted my book bag under my arms and made my way down the hall.

"How were Reis?"

"Okay," I replied. "He was scared at first but I showed him around."

I fairly bolted up the stairs to my room, and threw myself on the bed, unaccountably happier than I'd ever remembered myself being in my entire thirteen years.

Two weeks later, my mother collapsed in the bathroom, vomiting blood. Red poured out everywhere, from her mouth, her nose, between her legs. My grandmother called an ambulance while I sat with her, mopping her body with a towel, trying to keep the blood inside her so she wouldn't lose any more. When the ambulance arrived, I overheard one of the medics ask my mother how long she'd been throwing up blood. She told them she didn't remember, a long time.

In the hospital, she was given morphine through a tube in her hand. One of the doctors who periodically visited my mother's room finally asked my grandmother to come with him out in the hall. When he saw me following, he told me to go back and sit with my mother in case she woke up, but my grandmother said it was alright: Whatever he had to say, I was going to have to hear sooner or later.

So the doctor explained, in a low voice that sounded almost disappointed, that he wouldn't know for sure until he operated; but based on the X rays and his physical examination, things didn't look very good. The tumor in my mother's right breast, he said, was roughly the size of an orange.

She didn't wake up after the operation, but only lay pale in her hospital bed, barely breathing. Although the doctors and nurses who came by to look at her all remarked as gently as possible that it was just as well, given the amount of pain she'd probably feel if she were conscious, I had a hard time believing them. I'd like to have been able to tell her how sorry I was for the times I'd left her alone.

I'd like to have told her she was a terrific dancer.

It was strange seeing my friends, dressed in their coats and ties, at another funeral. Their parents prodded them to shake my hand, to go with me up to the coffin so we could kneel together and say prayers over my mother's body. They were a little reluctant to accompany me, and I wondered how much of their discomfort had to do with the simple morbidity of the place and time, and how much was directed at me.

I was now, technically, an orphan.

Reis stayed by my side almost the entire time, steering me away from adults struck suddenly kind, and occasionally conveying me outside to the back of the funeral parlor for a clandestine smoke. He showed a side of himself I hadn't seen or suspected—quiet, respectful—and without fully comprehending why, his very composure made me sadder even than the sight of my mother's waxy, emaciated body. As if the dust had finally settled after an explosion, revealing a scene of profound and irredeemable desolation. I found myself pulling cigarette smoke deep down into my lungs, feeling the pressure accumulating there, and slowly I begin to shake.

Reis kicked a stone and sent it rolling down the alley.

"It shits," he said.

"It really does," I agreed.

I wasn't sure what he meant, specifically: death, or sadness, or loss. He could have meant any of those things, or all of them together. Or something more essential for which we had no good words.

Reis spent the night of the funeral at my grandmother's house. He slept with me in my bed. It was uncomfortable at first; there was no room to move around and the heat of another body made me sweat. We remained awake long after my grandmother called upstairs for us to turn out the light, listening to the myriad small sounds strange bodies make. Each in our own way trying to find good words for the truth.

The Chase family has buried the dead of Putnam County for more than fifty years, so it seemed quite natural for me to engage the current proprietor for my grandmother's cremation. Now approaching the funeral parlor, I'm extremely grateful that Judith has agreed to come with me to collect the ashes. I'm afraid of doing something inappropriate while going through the paperwork—laughing when I should cry, perhaps, or crying when I ought to laugh. Whatever happens, I believe Judith will supply the balance just by being there.

Norton Chase stands up as we enter his office. It's a small room, crammed with the plush, solid kind of furniture typically displayed in bargain store windows. Chase himself is a tall man with a slight stoop, completely bald except for a few black hairs behind his ears. He has a splash of liver spots across one cheek, and his canine teeth stick out over his lower lip—an ambivalent touch, as if his sad and rather homely face masks a reservoir of specific cruelty.

He indicates a pair of salmon-colored chairs facing his desk, and once we're sitting, he opens the proceedings by saying he didn't know my grandmother, but that he understands she was a fine woman. To which I agree.

Then he slides a folder cross his desk, and while I'm looking over the invoice, he clears his throat and says, "I understand there's a plot already."

"Yes," I reply, distracted. "My grandfather's buried here."

"You don't wish to—ah—inter her there?"

I look up from the folder. Something in his tone makes me seethe: the slightly pompous *ah,* the way he says *inter* instead of *bury*. As if a polite word or two can excuse the indignity of death, the embarrassment of leaking bowels, flesh bloating like a poison apple.

"Actually," I tell him, "she wasn't much fond of this place."

An uncomfortable silence follows, and I realize almost immediately I've said the wrong thing. Like the bad boy in a fairy tale, I opened my mouth and a frog jumped out. No hope of retrieving it, either. It bounds across the room, too quick to catch. All I can do is let it go.

I bend back over the invoice, though not fast enough to miss Judith smiling an apology to the undertaker. Chase smiles back benignly, as if to say he's seen any number of cases like me and they're all, sadly, hopeless.

Once our business is concluded, Chase goes down the hall and returns with a small wooden box with a flat lid. It looks like a birdhouse, actually. Judith holds it on her knees in the car on the way back, but as I pull into her driveway she's suddenly unsure whether to put it on the floor or leave it on the seat.

She looks helplessly across at me, and the next minute we're laughing, uncontrollable, belly-aching laughter. The box bumps up and down her knees as she gasps, "I'm sorry, I'm sorry," between breaths.

It isn't clear who she's apologizing to.

The fit doesn't last very long, and when it's over, we both sit back, weak, a few last spasms of laughter rising to the surface.

"You know she shrank a lot as she got older," Judith says. "You could see her driving somewhere, and she was so little it looked like there wasn't anybody driving her car." She covers her eyes for a second. "I know it's terrible, but that's probably what I'm going to remember most clearly about her."

I nod, looking down at the box resting between us, balanced precariously on the little divider designed to hold coffee cups and spare change.

"What I remember is how she used to save scraps for all the stray dogs that used to wander through the neighborhood. She'd say it was a sin to waste good food, but I always had a sneaking suspicion she did it because she was sort of a stray herself. She had a sympathy that came from learning to live among strangers. Hell, even my grandfather was just a stranger she'd met on a farm somewhere in Czechoslovakia at the beginning of the war. In a pigsty, to be exact. Grandpa distracted the pigs while Grandma went through picking out anything that wasn't too rotten to eat. I have a feeling that was their wedding banquet."

"I'm not sure I'd have had the courage," Judith says, leaning her head back against the headrest.

"I'll bet they didn't think about it much. They were hungry, so they ate. They were cold so they slept together. Wondering if it was the right thing to do was probably a luxury they couldn't afford."

"You would have liked Kevin," Judith says after a moment. "The man I woke up for. I met him in the library, where he was researching some Indian mounds around here. A scholar from the university, over in Athens. You can imagine how excited I was, someone to talk to about other things than money and diapers and the mines. We met afternoons. For coffee first, the rest came later."

She smiles sadly, staring straight ahead.

"In my own house I was unfaithful to my husband, while the babies slept. After a year, Kevin asked me to marry him, to leave David and marry him. Who knows what I felt. It was like being outside of time, real love happening to me, in my life. Then Mitchell started crying in his crib and I got out of bed to pick him up, and then Colin woke up, too, and I sat holding both of them, which was another experience, just as powerful but full of time. Details. Mitchell had a rash and Colin was cranky from waking up too soon from his nap. I thought, here is this life going on around me, and it will keep going on even after I'm gone. Even if I were gone."

She turns now to look at me. At this angle, in this light, she looks ancient—weathered, like a stone or the trunk of a tree.

"It was a romantic decision," she continues. "I put Colin back to bed and carried the baby into the bedroom where Kevin was waiting for me under the covers, and told him I could never see him again. He didn't argue, he didn't ask why. I had a baby in my arms and that was enough. He put on his clothes while I sat watching on the bed, and then he asked if he could kiss me and I said no. The last I saw of him was from the doorway as he got into his car and drove away, and it was as if I'd suddenly been allowed to see down to the bottom of myself. Everything made sense, all the things I'd worried about and struggled over ever since I could remember."

She reaches over and pats my arm. "Luxuries are such poor, pale things," she says, smiling. "Hardly worth the trouble."

She sets the box on the seat as she gets out of the car. She studies it a moment before closing the door, then suggests that I put a seat belt around it in case I hit a patch of ice. The ashes might spill all over the car otherwise.

"No matter how little she cared what happened to her earthly remains," she says, "your grandma would probably not have liked the idea of ending up inside a vacuum cleaner."

When I get back to my grandmother's house, I find a dead rabbit on the front porch.

The fur around its neck is matted and caked with blood. A thin trickle of blood from its mouth has stained the snow bright red. Mesmerized, I stand studying various details, its placement by the kitchen door, the angle of the gash along its neck.

I can't tell what it's supposed to mean. Is it a warning? Or a gift?

Inside, the telephone starts ringing. Nudging the pathetic frozen corpse out of the way, I dig for my keys while I automatically start counting the number of rings. My mother used to say it was polite for the caller to allow the telephone to ring ten times in order to give the person on the other end enough time to get to the phone and answer. That was in the days before answering machines eliminated the need for such small politenesses, of course. Still, the habit of counting remains and I'm always a bit startled when the phone cuts off too quickly, answered by mechanical clicks and whirrings.

There's no answering machine connected to my grandmother's

telephone, however, and whoever is calling now—gives up prematurely on the seventh ring, seconds before I push open the door and stumble, swearing, into the kitchen.

The phone rings again almost immediately.

"Hello," Richard says, his voice staticky and far away.

"Did you just call a second ago?"

"Am I wrong, or is the proper form of return greeting still hello?" he asks.

I tell him hello—a bit testily—then repeat my question.

"Yes," he replies, "I thought I had the wrong number, so I hung up and tried again. Is there a problem?"

"No, no problem."

For half a second, I consider mentioning the dead rabbit on the porch. But then I'd have to tell him about the break-in, the mess in my bedroom, the figure on the bluff overlooking Potter Lake. And that would be just the beginning.

"I practically broke my neck trying to get inside, that's all," I say.

"Oh." He's quiet a minute. "Aren't you wondering why I called?"

The truth would probably hurt his feelings, so I tell him yes, I was wondering.

"I'm angry at you," he replies. "For the other night."

"You mean saying I was sorry."

"Yes."

A familiar process starts up, like a hinge springing open at the top of my head. But this time I'm ready for it, and I pull the lid down before anything has a chance to slip out. I am, after all, clutching a box with my grandmother's ashes in it and someone has gone through the trouble of slaughtering a rabbit on my front porch.

The time for detachment, it seems, has past.

"Well, what about it?" I ask.

Something in my tone seems to cause Richard to reconsider his approach. "I didn't think it was fair," he says a bit defensively. "To just spring something like that on a person and then hang up."

"Fair."

"Right."

Once, when I was small, my father had taken me down inside a shaft mine, just to show me what it was like. Within a hundred feet the black walls closed around us and the air turned thick and sooty. The only illumination came from the light on my father's hardhat and the special lamp he carried, called a permissible lamp. He told me to watch its flame very carefully. If it started to burn low, there wasn't enough oxygen in the shaft and we'd suffocate; if it burned too high, there was methane, which meant the mine was about to blow up.

I've often wondered since then whether a steady flame meant that the air was clean and good to breathe or—as I believe is more likely—that all the poisons had simply managed to strike a perfect, if ephemeral, balance.

"I think you're right Richard," I reply. "I think it was up to you to apologize for sleeping around before I apologized for being a crappy lover. I guess I was trying to kill two birds with one stone, and that was wrong."

I can almost hear his mind spinning on the other end.

"I gather you're not going to deny anything I've just said," I add.

His voice comes through very small and clogged. "No."

"Good. At least that's settled."

"So where do we go from here?" he asks.

Before I can come up with an answer, it hits me that there might not be one—at least not a simple or direct one. It's possible that the air that's good to breathe is also the air that's full of poisons.

"I don't know, Richard. Let me finish here first, and then I'll come home and we'll sort this out. I can only manage one mess at a time."

"I don't think we've made a mess, exactly."

But I don't want to argue. I'm suddenly aware of being worn out in a way that a good night's sleep won't cure. I want to finish up here as quickly as possible and then go home.

"I'll call you tomorrow," I promise.

For lack of a better place I set the box of ashes on the oak buffet. It seems appropriate; my grandmother spent more time in the kitchen than anywhere else. She was a good cook, she liked to bake, and I liked the smell of it: bread, cakes, nut rolls for Easter and Christmas. This is the smell I miss in her house now.

Once, she'd put too much of something in the nut rolls—yeast or flour, I can't remember which—and when she opened the oven door to check their progress, the rolls were literally crawling across the pans and down the sides of the oven. She sat on the floor, laughing, covering her mouth with her hands. When I came in to see what was going on, she could only point at the oven, at the rolls wriggling around like fat, golden snakes.

She had a knack for seeing the humor in disaster.

I'd already done some packing before heading out to the funeral parlor, and now the second round seems to go more quickly. Most of the work involves clearing out the basement, throwing out old jars of canned fruits and vegetables and testing old electrical appliances to see if they work.

Every once in a while I find it necessary to get away from all the dust and mildew, and during one break I drag a box of old photographs upstairs, to sort them at the kitchen table over a strong cup of coffee. The top layer consists mostly of black-and-white pictures of people long dead. Their faces seem stoic and graceful, as if the cameras in those days had the power to look beyond what was transient to something more substantial. Later photographs seem almost obscene in their full-color detail, showing people caught in mid-gesture, plastic cups in their hands, shoveling cake in their mouths.

Somewhere in the middle of the pile I come across two pictures stuck together front to back. The bottom one turns out to be a yellowed Ektachrome of Reis and me standing on my grandmother's porch, showing off the new winter coats we've gotten for Christmas.

It takes awhile to figure out why the picture bothers me so much. At first I think it's the smart-ass grins on our faces, the absurd sense of happiness. I want to scream at the two boys in the picture, to warn them of the danger. But they wouldn't hear me even if they could. It's not easy as children to understand the violence that comes from even casual gestures.

A layer of snow suddenly breaks away from the ledge over the kitchen window, and crashes to the ground. The noise is like a brick hitting a wall. After my heart starts beating normally again, and I sit back down in my chair, I realize what it is that really disturbs me about the picture.

It's the coat Reis has on, a dark blue parka, like the man on the bluff over Potter Lake.

Without knowing how, I suddenly find myself standing on the front porch, shivering, straining to see clearly up the dark street.

He was just here a minute ago, I'm sure of it.

Which way did he go?

Dammit Reis, I want to shout, *what's the point of hiding now?*

A college professor once told me that every lie is its own truth. He was not one of my professors, actually, but a patient. Still, it remains an interesting lesson, of which I was reminded after Stephen began telling me his dreams. He would sit on the couch with his hands folded in his lap, describing angels climbing a ladder to the stars; a funnel of smoke chugging between the carcasses of dead animals;

seven cows drinking at a river. One night, he told me, three vines burst into bloom in his hands.

He made an effort to make each dream sound original—squinting, sighing, revising the images as they came to him. I wondered what was going to happen when he ran out of Bible stories. Where would he turn next, or would he simply get tired of the game?

After three weeks, I asked him what the word *dream* meant.

A foolish grin spread across his face.

"Like where they're supposed to come from and shit?" he asked.

I shook my head and laid my pad and pencil down on the ottoman in front of my chair. It was late June, the air conditioner in my office wasn't working right; my scalp felt damp and sweat made wide rings under the arms of my shirt. I imagined myself melting, coming apart, only a matter of time before my fingers dripped off and my arms plopped like hot wax onto the floor.

"No," I replied. "To you. What does the word mean to you?"

Stephen blinked, his white eyelashes fluttering like moth wings. A line of sweat trickled down his face. He ran his fingers through his hair.

"I don't know doc. They're from the unconscious and shit, right? Like the stuff people see in the day that gets stuck in their heads without them paying attention, and it gets mixed up with all the shit they don't even know about themselves. The real crazy shit, like they want to do things to their mothers and kill their fathers. Right?"

It occurred to me that he might not be telling me what he really thought, but only what he'd heard or read somewhere. Yet as I listened, a germ of an idea presented itself: He was speaking in code. A crude and obvious symbolism, perhaps, but probably the only code he understood well enough to use.

In a language of borrowed dreams, he was trying to tell me something.

"Hey doc," he asked, "am I right?"

He had sat forward on the couch, elbows on his knees, leaning toward me. Something in his pose—the combination of eagerness and cockiness—unnerved me. For the briefest of moments, I was aware of regarding him as something other than a patient. Then a kind of dizziness washed over me, not unlike vertigo, where the danger was not of being pushed but of falling, of choosing to fall.

I wiped a hand over my face and forced myself to smile. "Yes," I replied. "That's exactly right, Stephen."

The well of dreams dried up after that, but something new took its place.

We could talk.

Stephen discussed with me his decision to go back to high school in the fall, even though it meant starting his junior year again and being a year older than everyone else in his class. At first, he approached the idea a little smugly, as though his age would give him an advantage over the rest of his classmates. Later in the session, he told me he was actually embarrassed about being older. He was afraid the other kids would talk about him behind his back. Being talked about, he muttered, was the thing he hated most in the world.

I'd have liked to pursue that, but it was clear from the way he squirmed that the subject made him extremely uncomfortable. I didn't want to exacerbate him any further. The rapport between us still felt fragile.

He was able to speak much more freely about his part-time job as a clerk in one of the grocery stores in his neighborhood in Washington Heights. He hated his supervisor, a man he called the Pothole, because his face was covered with acne scars. His coworkers were all so stupid they couldn't tell Campbell's soup from tuna fish, but for some reason he always ended up catching the blame for their mistakes. The Pothole constantly accused him of being clumsy, lazy, and untrustworthy.

Consequently, the Pothole was an ass.

One afternoon, Stephen pulled a squashed package out of a greasy paper bag and tossed it across the room so that it landed on my lap. It was a single serving of lemon pie.

"Don't say I never brung you nothing," he said.

"I'm touched, Stephen," I replied. "Thank you."

"Yeah, well. It's a onetime thing, don't get used to it."

It was high summer, and he'd arrived wearing shorts and a T-shirt. His body had begun to fill out, and it crossed my mind that he might be showing more of himself as a deliberate provocation. He sat now with his arms at his sides and his legs spread. There were several purple marks on his legs, and a few on his arms. I couldn't tell if they were burns or bruises, but when I asked about them, Stephen made a face and said he didn't remember where he'd gotten them. He'd gone out a few nights before, he said.

"Where'd you go?"

He shrugged. "Just out."

"By yourself, or with friends?"

"I met some people."

"Did you have a good time?"

He squinted and flashed me an odd leer, which on another person might have looked a little frightening. Stephen looked like he was trying on something that was obviously the wrong size.

"Not the kind of good time you'd like," he replied.

For some reason, the remark amused me.

"What would I like?" I asked.

In response, he brought a fist to his mouth and made a crude gesture. Then he dropped his hand back to his lap.

"Why do you think that's what I'd like?"

"What do you think, I'm going to fall for that kind of question?"

He smiled and leaned back into the couch. "For a guy who's supposed to be smart, you sure act dumb."

If nothing else, I thought, at least his confidence was increasing. I'd never seen him so relaxed.

The following week, just before I was to leave for my August vacation, he announced that he'd had another dream.

"Do you want to tell me about it?" I asked.

He struggled for a while. The only thing he could remember was a man in a room, dressed in a raincoat.

"Do you have any idea who it might be?" I asked.

Instead of answering, he pulled on a string that was coming loose from the arm of the couch, and wrapped it around his index finger. The tip of the finger slowly turned pink, then scarlet, then purple. At the same time, an erection had risen in his shorts.

I glanced at it and then, embarrassed, glanced away. As if doing so would have changed anything. When I looked back, Stephen was smiling, a smart-alecky, boyish grin.

He said the man's name was Chester.

But when I asked who Chester was, he only shook his head.

"How do you know the man's name is Chester then?"

Stephen relaxed the tension on the string, but didn't unwind it completely. Gradually, the lurid accretion of blood in his fingertip abated.

"He was wearing a raincoat," he replied finally.

"I don't understand."

Stephen delicately shifted his weight on the couch, tilting his pelvis very slightly forward.

"Chester the Molester," he said, his tone implying the answer should be obvious.

"That's a childhood term, isn't it?"

"Yeah. You know, the type that hides around corners with his pants down."

He gripped the string once more, hard, and the tip of his finger began its slow transformation again.

"Have you ever met anyone like that?" I asked, softly. "In the past I mean, before this particular dream."

"Not what I know of."

"How about recently?"

He waited a long time before replying. In the silence, he grinned, but it was no boyish smile; there was nothing in it of heartbreak or innocence or childhood.

"What do you think doc?" he replied.

Stephen did not resume our weekly sessions after I returned from vacation. His mother called to say that, between school starting and his part-time job at the grocery store, he'd be too busy. She thanked me, though, for whatever help I'd given her son.

He was completely back to normal now, she said, praise the Lord.

I wasn't sure whether to feel relieved or disappointed.

I didn't see him again for several months.

One morning, shortly before Christmas, I found him crouching outside the building on Ninety-sixth Street where my office is. He sat just outside the awning, shivering and damp from the snow melting on his head and shoulders. The doorman had refused to let him wait for me inside the foyer, and it wasn't hard to understand why. The light coat he had on was torn and stained with blood, and his face was bruised in several places. He held an empty coffee cup between his battered hands. As I approached the building, I'd thought he was just another panhandler looking for change.

When I got him inside, I called a deli on the corner and ordered two large coffees. He didn't want anything to eat, which wasn't surprising, since his mouth was swollen. I offered him a blanket I kept on the back of my chair, and after he wrapped himself in it and gradually stopped shivering, I asked him what had happened.

"I was out," he mumbled.

"Out where?" I tried to sound calm and impartial. "Alone or with other people?"

"Both," he replied.

The doorman buzzed to let me know that the coffee had arrived, and I went out to the office waiting room to pay the delivery boy. When I came back, Stephen had let the blanket slip off his shoulders and the color was coming back into his face. I handed him his coffee. He had a hard time pulling up the plastic tab on the lid, and even after he managed it, he took only a couple of sips. The coffee seemed to burn his mouth.

"It's good money," he said then. "Better than I was making at the grocery store, that's for sure."

Outside my window came the laughter and shouting of a gang of children on their way down Central Park West, headed for school. Then they passed and there was only the noise of morning traffic.

"Especially from the older guys," Stephen said. "Rich guys from Jersey, Connecticut. They pay more for under eighteen."

I waited awhile to see if he was going to add anything else.

"Do they hurt you?" I asked.

He tried to shrug, but the effort cost him.

"Doesn't hurt," he replied.

"What do you tell your parents? I imagine you're out quite late sometimes."

"I don't live home no more. Not for a couple of months."

I nodded, wondering if his mother had lied to me about Stephen being too busy with school and work. Or had she really been hopeful? It would have been grim for her either way, I supposed.

I asked Stephen where he was living now.

"Places," he replied. He pulled the lid off the coffee cup and blew on the coffee, then took one or two tentative sips. "Everything's a deal, doc. You got something to give, you got someplace to live." He took several long swallows of coffee then, draining the contents. Then he sat for a moment, tapping the empty cup on the arm of the couch. When he spoke again, he was still staring at the cup.

"I was wondering maybe I could make a deal with you."

I swallowed the spit that had collected in my mouth. "What kind of deal do you mean?"

I thought we might sit there forever before he answered. When he finally did reply, there was neither anger nor connivance in his voice.

"Got no place to stay, doc. Nothin' to eat. Can't go nowhere."

I looked down at my hands, folded in my lap. "Let's think this through," I said. "Maybe together we can come up with a better solution."

An abject look crossed the boy's face. His shoulders sagged and he looked close to tears.

"Take me home with you, doc."

"I can't do that, Stephen."

"Man, it's cold. It's wet."

"I can't. There are boundaries between client and therapist. Practical boundaries. Ethical boundaries. Stepping past them would do more harm than good, believe me."

The boy would not stop looking at me, his expression a void beyond misery or complaint.

"What I *can* do," I continued "is help you find a safe place to stay while we figure out what you want to do next."

"I can't go back home."

I told him that he wouldn't have to, but that for the next few nights, at least, he needed a warm bed and decent meals and a chance to think things over. I told him I knew people who could help, people whose job it was to help find places for young men in his situation.

Once he agreed to this plan, I asked him if he wouldn't mind waiting in the outer room while I made a few phone calls. There was a couch out there were he could sit, and magazines to keep himself occupied. If he wanted, I could order more coffee or something to eat.

He declined the coffee.

On his way out the door, he stopped and turned.

"I know things that could make you feel real good," he said.

As kindly as I could I told him that was the last thing on my mind.

After twenty minutes on the phone with various agencies, I managed to find him a place in a youth shelter on the West Side; but when I went out to the waiting room to give him the news, he was gone.

He never returned.

Norton Chase smiles when I return to the funeral parlor.

"So, you've had a change of heart about the resting place?" he says, rising from behind his desk to shake my hand.

"Not exactly," I reply, taking the seat he offers. "I was hoping you might be able to help me with something else."

"Another sad occasion?"

"No. Well, yes, in a way. The mother of a friend of mine passed away five years ago. I haven't been able to find him and I was wondering if you might have a record of his address. Some way to get in contact with him."

Chase blinks and sucks on his bottom lip.

"You've tried all the usual ways of finding him?"

"Of course."

"Mr. Fowler." He looks down at his knobby hands and brushes the nail of one thumb with the back of the other. "The records here are confidential."

"I'd be willing to pay."

"That wouldn't be appropriate."

"Can you at least tell me when she died? The date?"

"I imagine it would be on file with the county."

"But now that I'm here, it would save me a trip."

Chase bends his head one way and then another, as if the effort of weighing his decision requires some sort of physical expression. "What would the name of the deceased be?" he asks.

"Paley. Roberta Paley."

He purses his lips, nods, then stands up and leaves the room. While I wait for him to return, I study a print on the wall, a reproduction of an Arcadian landscape, rosy peasants resting among the ruins of a classical temple. The frame is painted gold, and the texture of the brush strokes has been preserved in the print to create the illusion of an original. I hear Chase coming back down the hall; he stops just next to my chair, a manila folder in his hand.

"This is very interesting, Mr. Fowler," he says. "The receipt for Mrs. Paley's arrangements seems to have been made out to your grandmother." He passes me the folder. "The file contains a copy of Mrs. Paley's obituary, but I don't see any mention of a son." He rubs his thumb and forefinger reflexively up and down his windpipe. "Perhaps . . ."

"No."

I scan the announcement, close the file, and hand it back to him. "He's alive," I say. "I'm sure of it."

When I was a boy, the Fairview Library had been a one-story building on Oak Street, next to the post office. This building has been turned into a veterinary clinic, and the receptionist, who seems bored and unfazed by the number of cats crawling around her feet, gives me directions to the new library.

The library isn't really new, though. It's merely been transferred to the shell of St. Barnabas Catholic church, which sits on top of a hill looking down on Fairview. A new church has been built on the other side of the St. Barnabas parking lot. It's an ugly, white monolith with a sloping roof and complex stained glass windows. After studying the windows for a few minutes, I can't tell what the scenes are supposed to be.

The old church—the library—could easily serve as the model for every Christmas store window display and tiny-town train set I've ever seen. It's made of red brick, and has a steeple. The cross has been taken down, of course, but the vines spreading up along the walls remain intact. In the windows, I can clearly make out scenes from the Stations of the Cross: the wicked centurions flogging Christ, St. Veronica offering her miraculous hankie.

In the foyer, there's a long coat rack against one wall, and a long rubber mat for boots. I push through the swinging doors into the main room. A clear plastic runner runs from the doors to the librarian's desk, situated directly below what used to be the choir loft.

The librarian looks to be about sixty, with dyed black hair and a round, pleasant face. She has on a print dress, a long-sleeved cardigan, and a strand of amber-colored beads. I ask her if the library keeps back issues of the local papers on microfilm.

"Yes," she replies worriedly, almost as if my question were mildly inappropriate. "What issues might you be interested in looking at?"

I tell her I want to see everything over the past ten years. As she digests this request, her expression becomes vaguely concerned and she begins unconsciously rubbing one of her amber-colored beads between her fingers. Then she nods and disappears into a room behind her desk, leaving the door open.

While I'm waiting, a boy pushes through the swinging doors. He's dressed in a bulky coat and a bright blue, knitted cap that hangs down to his shoulders, like a nightcap. His glasses, in thick brown plastic frames, are almost completely fogged over. He comes loping over to the desk next to me, and hefts a pair of oversize books covered in stiff plastic film out of his knapsack. He looks up, squinting through the fogged lenses, and smiles.

"Waiting long?" he asks.

"Not too long."

"Good."

The boy wipes his nose on the sleeve of his jacket and then examines the sleeve. A small clot of mucous sticks there, just above the wrist. Immediately, he bends his arm back behind him and tries to rub the offense on the back of his jacket. At the same time, I turn away, pretending to look at the clock over the desk. Then the librarian comes back, carrying several small white cardboard boxes. She sees the boy and smiles.

"Gary," she says. "You're a day late on each of those, I think."

"I know," the boy says, attempting to sound sorrier than I suspect he actually is.

The librarian sets the boxes down on the desk and takes both books from the boy. She opens each one, looking inside the front cover of each and nodding.

"Uh-oh," she says. "Two days late. You want to put that to account or pay it now?"

"I'll pay it," the boy says. He wrestles twenty cents from his pocket and slaps it on the counter.

"You want your receipt?"

The boy shakes his head. "I trust you."

He lopes back along the plastic runner to the swinging doors, then turns and waves back at the librarian. Then he's gone.

She watches him go. "My grandnephew," she confides, with a wink, then slides the white cardboard boxes across the desk. "The rules say you can only sign out two spools at a time." She leans forward and lowers her voice confidentially, smiling. "But I think that's bullshit. Just more work for everybody. You just take these five rolls now, and when you're through bring them back and I'll give you five more if you need."

"Thank you."

She waves her hand, deprecating. "It's just bullshit," she says again, as if she enjoys this small infraction of propriety.

I carry the boxes to a cubicle at the back of the library, away from the windows. It takes a few minutes to thread the machine so that the film appears right-side up on the screen; then I begin searching the arrest announcements at the back of every edition, beginning with the most recent issues. An hour passes before I find what I'm looking for, in an issue two years old: *Reis Paley, for reckless driving and bodily injury to another person.*

I have to read the address twice, though, because it doesn't make sense. I scan back another year and a half. Reis's name appears twice more—once for shoplifting, once for drunk driving.

Both times, the address is the same.

My tires spray slush as I turn down Judith's street. Gray pools of melting snow fill the road, and ice drips off the trees I pass along the way. The front yards are all brown and muddy.

Judith comes to the door wearing yellow rubber gloves. Her face is flushed and shiny, and she's wearing a pair of jeans and a button-down shirt with the sleeves rolled up. The shirt is missing a pocket and hangs off her thin frame: one of her husband's castoffs, I think.

"Were you waiting long?" she asks, breathless. "I was upstairs bleaching the bathroom grout. Such a romantic life I lead." She laughs.

"He lived at Grandma's."

Judith shakes her head, and wipes a line of sweat off her face with her arm. "I'm sorry. Who? What?"

I'm still standing on the front porch. "Reis. He lived at Grandma's. It's her address in the arrest reports."

"Ah," Judith replies. Her mouth becomes a fine, thin line. "Do you want to come in?"

"I want to know why you didn't tell me."

"Come in, Chris. I'd rather not waste money heating the whole neighborhood."

She steps back to let me pass through, and then closes the door. She turns and sees me standing with my arms folded across my chest.

"You can take your coat off," she says.

"I want to know why you didn't tell me."

"Is that the price of good manners?"

"Why are you avoiding my question?"

She sighs. "The last time you were here, you asked me where he is now. I didn't think it was important where he lived before."

She walks past me, heading up the stairs.

"I have to finish the bathroom. If you want to come up, please take off your boots."

I'm tempted to follow right away, tracking mud and slush all over the carpet. Instead, I take off my boots and put them on the tray in the hall.

Judith is kneeling on the bathroom floor, scrubbing the tile with a brush. The room reeks of Clorox.

"You should have a fan in here," I tell her. "The fumes aren't good for you."

"I've been doing this for twenty years."

For a long while, there's nothing but the sound of the brush scraping across the floor.

"I'm not sure I believe you didn't think it was important," I tell her, as gently as I can.

"Mm." She pushes the brush hard along the grout between two tiles. "I suppose the word *jealousy* never occurred to you."

"Jealousy of whom?"

"Don't be obtuse."

She stops scrubbing long enough to wipe the sweat off her face; then she resumes work.

"So tell me, are you—" she pauses briefly, struggling to rephrase the question— "Is there someone you're together with now? Would you say boyfriend? I'm sorry, I don't know what to call it."

The silence between us holds nearly a minute

"I've lived with Richard for ten years now. He's a doctor."

She nods, absorbing this information.

"Tell me how you love him."

"Why?"

"Because I want to know," she says simply. "I want to understand. For myself. How you can do what you think is wrong and still live with yourself."

"I don't think it's wrong."

My words hang in the air, flimsy things, hardly effective against the armor of her silence. They flutter to the floor, like soot, like ashes. Judith might easily scrub them away with her brush.

"He lives in Egypt Bottom," she says finally. "There's an empty house there, three or four miles back in the woods."

"Yes," I reply, "I know it."

Halfway down the stairs, I realize there's something I've forgotten to ask. Judith seems surprised to see me back. At any rate, she's simply kneeling on the floor, holding the scrub brush in her lap. She looks up when I stop in the doorway.

"How long did he live with Grandma?" I ask.

Judith blinks several times, as if attempting to make sense of a language not her own. She raises one shoulder a fraction of an inch and lets it fall.

"He was still young," she says. "Eighteen, nineteen." She goes back to scrubbing the floor. "He kept getting into trouble after you left, you know, and it just got worse. I suppose his mother just got tired of it and told him to get out."

The trouble had started before I left, though.

A few weeks after my mother's funeral, Reis was suspended for smoking in the boy's bathroom at school. Not long after that—though he'd taken the precaution of opening his window and blow-ing the smoke outside—his mother caught him smoking in his bedroom. Then crazy Oleg at the package store turned him in for stealing a package of cupcakes. Roberta kept a closer eye on him after that, which was how she discovered the magazines hidden between his box spring and mattress.

They were cheap newsprint, full of grainy, black-and-white photographs of people touching themselves or each other, and stories full of words like *fucking*. Of course, I knew what *fucking* meant, and *balls, titties, dick*. Other words were more obscure. *Snatch. Pud. Woodie.* I could only figure them out by the way they were used, and when that failed I had to ask Reis; which I didn't like to do, because ignorance in such matters was equivalent to immaturity. And at thirteen, there was no worse crime than being immature.

Oddly enough, I didn't find myself getting aroused by any of the pictures. If I imagined myself alone in a room with any of the people in them, nothing happened. What I enjoyed was looking, the thrill and terror of gazing at things normally hidden. I suddenly understood all the fuss about sin. The suspense was exhilarating, the risk of getting caught balanced against the idea of getting away with something.

It was probably the danger that gave me my first *woodie*—that, and sharing the risk with Reis. I'm not sure that sinning alone would have been half as much fun. We turned the danger into a kind of code: *I got a woodie in English class today,* we'd say, or *My pud needs a rub.*

When Roberta found Reis's collection of magazines, she decided to start going back to church. On the first Sunday of Lent, she and Reis sat beside my grandmother and me, watching Father Wood go through the motions of Mass. Sometimes he'd forget what he was saying in mid-sentence and one of the altar boys would have to prompt him. He'd mumble the communion blessing, dropping the wafer into our hands while muttering something that sounded like

Buy cries. Reis and I would mumble back, *Pay men,* then walk solemnly back to our pew to kneel with our hands over our faces, pretending to pray.

After the final hymn, we were free. One Sunday, we hopped on our bicycles and rode to Egypt Bottom, because Reis thought we should break into the shack where the family had been murdered a few years earlier.

"Maybe we'll find some clues," he said.

There was nothing to break into, however. The front door hung open on rusty hinges, and the bits of glass or plastic that covered the windows had long since been stolen. Reis and I paced through the rooms looking for signs of struggle, but the bloodstains had already faded along with the chalk lines that had marked the spots where the bodies had lain. Mice skittered loudly across the floors and windowsills, and the smell of their nests and droppings permeated the air. A fine silt of dust lay over everything, thinner in patches where things had been stolen more recently. Even the stove and refrigerator had been torn out and carted away.

We picked our way up the splintery planks that led up to the second story. The beds were gone; burned, probably, having been soaked with blood. Snow and rain had rotted the floor of the front room, and neither Reis nor I felt brave enough to try the buckled boards.

In the back room, we found a small wooden box with four sticks in it. Each stick had a crude face drawn on in pencil, and a piece of cloth tacked underneath. It was impossible to tell if they were supposed to be boy dolls or girl dolls, or some combination of the two.

Reis carried the box to the window and pulled out an egg-crusted spider web. Tilting the box toward the light, he showed me pencil markings on the inside, apparently representing a table and chairs, a stove, a couch, and beds.

A few seconds later, he started to pull the frame apart.

"Don't," I said, holding his hands.

"Why?"

"It was somebody's."

"So?"

"Somebody went to trouble."

"So?"

"So let it be."

He shook his head and sighed. "You got funny ideas sometimes, little brother."

Nevertheless, he handed the box over to me. I carefully replaced the stick dolls, which rattled inside as I set the box down on the floor where we'd found it.

Reis pulled two cigarettes out of his jacket pocket. He passed one to me and we sat by the window smoking. The window frame was set low enough in the wall so we could look outside without straining our necks. Most of what we saw were trees, whose trunks, wet with spring rain, looked almost black. Something like a clearing surrounded the house itself, though, with an upside-down rocking chair sticking out of the muddy ground.

After a few minutes, I broached a subject that had been bothering me for several days.

"You never said the boy that drowned was your cousin," I ventured. "Kid at school had to tell me."

Reis blew some smoke through his nose. "You believe him?"

"Don't have any reason not to."

"Don't have any reason to, neither."

We finished our cigarettes and crushed the butts on the floor, leaving black stains on the wood. Reis stretched his legs out, resting the back of his head against the wall and closing his eyes. After a few minutes, it seemed like he'd fallen asleep; but when I spoke his name, he opened his eyes, alert and shining as a cat's.

"I don't see the big deal," he muttered.

"Just that you could of told me the whole truth."

Reis shut his eyes again, and clamped his lips together. He started knocking the back of his head against the wall, harder and harder, until I kicked at his leg and told him to stop. He quit, but still kept his eyes shut.

"He weren't much younger except a year," he said finally "Spoiled like a baby and always hanging around. Everyone thought it was funny the way he hounded after me, till he got drowned, and then they all said I should of been watching him better. They didn't know how weird he was, neither." A nervous smile flickered across his lips. "Probably wouldn't believe the kinds of things he wanted to do."

"Maybe I would."

"What else the kid at school tell you?"

"I don't remember."

"Who was it said?"

"Dana Pulaski. The one you shot pool with down in his basement. He said you started acting goofy on him."

"It's a lie!" Reis opened his eyes wide and stuck his chin forward. The gesture lacked ferocity, though. "It was him that started it."

We sat.

"It's a damned lie," he said once more, miserably.

For a second, his face drained of all its toughness and certainty. I glanced at the window, thinking what I'd seen was a trick of the light, a thickening of clouds perhaps. But the change came and went so quickly, it couldn't have been a cloud; just as what Dana had told me couldn't have been a lie.

Reis tried to lift himself off the floor, but his body seemed to have turned to rubber. Only his eyes moved from side to side, and then they, too, grew still. Muddy gray light sifted through the window. Reis hugged his arms around himself to keep from shivering.

"Let's go," I said after a while, holding out my hand to help him up.

A thin gray mist had risen from the spongy ground around the house. It had begun to rain, too, pinpricks we hardly noticed until we reached the lip of the valley and it began to come down in sheets. Reis and I stood huddling under an elm that was just breaking leaves. Rain washed down on us and plastered our clothes to our bodies.

We waited a long time until a truck came down the road and stopped for us. We threw our bicycles in the bed and climbed in the cab with a gasp of thanks to the driver, laughing and sputtering like ordinary boys, riding away from the valley without so much as a look behind.

I'm driving much too quickly along the same road now, trying to beat the sunset. The road curves one way and then the other, past bald hills and naked trees, and hapless little shacks that even winter twilight fails to dignify. Out of the creeping dark appears an ancient barn, on the side of which I can just make out a faded green and white billboard: CHEW MAIL POU H TOBACC ! A mile later, there's a field where stalks of yellow grass poke their heads out of snow already singed black with coal dust. In the middle of it, as if dropped there by a careless giant, stand the ruins of a factory whose few remaining windows catch the last red rays of sunset.

Abruptly, the road veers downward and Egypt Bottom appears on my right. It looks desolate in the twilight, bare branches clattering in the wind like a gossip of old bones. The trails are packed with snow, impossible to drive through. I pull my car along the shoulder and get out, and before I've gone twenty yards, wet snow has soaked through my boots.

I can still recognize the landmarks after twenty-five years: a frozen pond, a bare hillock, a rusting silver trailer shaped like a zeppelin. A litter of broken things pokes through the snow in front of the trailer now, and a snapped clothesline swings blindly from a nearby tree. Whoever lives there will probably ignore me as long as I keep my distance, though they'd certainly mark my passage. Long ago, Reis had told me I'd be hopeless as a tracker, the way I crashed through the woods.

That had been in a different set of woods, of course, somewhere in the hills of West Virginia, where my Uncle Patrick had taken us on a weekend camping trip. It was our chance to get away from the *womenfolk,* as he called them. *The gaggle of geese. The clucking hens.* Funny names that had no meanness in them.

Uncle Patrick had no interest in either fishing or hunting, which came as a profound relief to me. Instead, we spent the weekend simply hiking through the woods. Uncle Patrick quizzed us on our knowledge of trees, birds, and insects. He seemed not to mind our nearly complete ignorance in these matters; in fact, he seemed to enjoy telling us that pine trees depended on the wind to fertilize their seeds, that most bees were female, that the proper name for a blue jay was *Cyanocitta cristata.*

We'd waited till he was asleep to sneak away, creeping almost on tiptoe through the dark as we picked our way over stones, branches, and fallen leaves. I held my breath, every muscle taut, at least until we put enough distance between us and the tent where Uncle Patrick lay sleeping. Reis was better at sneaking through the woods than I was. Every few yards I'd miss something that snapped under my feet.

Finally, we reached the small river we'd seen earlier in the day. From bank to bank, it was only fifteen yards across. When we'd passed by in daylight, the water had appeared mossy green; now it shimmered inky and opaque under a bright half-moon. The current was broken by three huge stones, whose gray backs stood out of the water at roughly even intervals between the banks.

"Doesn't look very deep," I whispered.

"Doesn't have to be. It's deep enough. Cold as hell, too, I'll bet."

I walked close to the shore. The water wasn't quite as dark there, and the riverbed glittered, a mosaic of colored stones. When I dipped my toes in, the hair on the back of my neck stood out and goose bumps rose up and down my arms. It was cold as hell, alright.

Reis strode past me while I stood there with the water lapping at my feet. I had a glimpse of his body merging soundlessly with the water, a pale creation of lights and shadows that abruptly disappeared. A rush, a ripple, some bubbles, and Reis came up in the middle of the river. Or his head did anyway, hair slicked down over his forehead. He turned to look at me, treading water.

I backed away a few feet, pulled off my T-shirt, and dropped it on the ground. I unzipped my shorts and slid them down, lifting first one leg out and then kicking with the other. They landed right on top of my T-shirt. I stood a moment just looking out at the river. In full sun, my arms and legs were tan, but the moonlight turned them nearly white. Thin as sticks, too.

Reis disappeared underwater and surfaced again farther downstream, turning back once more, waiting. I hesitated a fraction of a second longer, then slid my underpants down my legs. A breeze blew across my body, a ghostly hand, fragrant. I came back down to the water's edge, waded to where the riverbed dropped, and plunged gasping into the cold, clean dark.

We didn't stay in the water very long. Afterward, we stretched out on the opposite shore, hidden from the trail by the closest of the three boulders. A web of bluish stars hung over our heads, and off to the left, the moon.

Reis stretched close to me, the sharp points of his rib cage offered to the sky, his thigh curving neatly toward his hip. Pain shot behind my eyes and in my throat, and suddenly I was full of chatter, inane ideas, nervous thoughts, afraid to leave any silence between us. If there were silence, I might be persuaded to do something that might be better not to do. Better to live in the idea of a more perfect opportunity.

"I wonder how come you can't be tanned by the moon?" I asked.

"Why would you want to be?"

"It's light, isn't it?"

"Ain't hot enough."

"It would be a neat thing. A moontan. I wonder what color it would be?"

"You can't get one," Reis replied, "so why even think about it?"

"Would you turn blue?"

"Na, brown. Just like a suntan."

"Think about it, Reis. We could invent a whole new bunch of things. We could be rich. Moontan lotion."

"Moonglasses."

"Moondials."

"Moon baths."

"Ice cream moondaes."

Reis yawned, stretched again, and slid even closer. With less than an inch of space between us, it seemed almost as if a current shuddered between our two bodies, a perilous voltage, attractive and repellent at the same time. My mind went still, completely still, I could never say for sure then or later how the current finally leapt. All I knew was that my hand moved without seeming to move at all. It was the stillness in my head that moved, silence in the form of my hand that slid over Reis's leg, the wiry few hairs.

To touch him wailed in my head, forked down my arms and legs, and rolled like strange fruit along the roof of my mouth, the exotic taste of a new language, which in precisely the same moment became flesh and touched me, too.

Afterward I turned on my side to gaze at him resting now with his eyes closed. His face looked surprisingly innocent, like the children in the illustrated stories I'd long ago read aloud to old Mrs. Hodge. For a while, I thought this angelic blankness was a trick of the moonlight. Then I realized it was his real face, which I'd never noticed before because I'd always seen him under the enchantment of all the brave things he'd said and the way he'd always acted so certain of himself.

A profound sadness stole over me as I realized that the enchantment was broken.

From then on, I would always be afraid of drowning.

Even in the fading light, I can see some repairs have been made to the shack. Patches of glass or plastic have been laid in previously empty windows, a set of steps has been erected outside the front door. Timbers prop up both sides of the shack itself. There's a truck parked a couple of yards away and footprints scar the snow around it.

I step up to the door and knock.

And wait.

It's fully dark now, and cold. The moon has not begun to rise.

After a minute, I knock again, listening more keenly for any sounds that might give away an inhabitant on the other side of the door.

The silence from within the house is more complete than anything I've heard before.

Deeply disappointed, I come down off the stairs and take a few hesitant steps back toward the direction from which I'd come.

"You'd still make a lousy tracker," Reis says, behind me.

I turn back around, barely able to make him out, a deeper darkness in the yawning dark of the open door.

"I could hear you comin' from the road, practically," he adds.

I step back up to the door and for a long moment we stand looking over and through each other, grown men now, survivors of separate wars. Then Reis slides back into the dark interior of the shack and motions me to follow.

"Sit," he says, when we get back to the kitchen.

The only light is a kerosene lantern on a table littered with crusty plates, cups, and empty bottles. On top of the counter sits a Coleman camp stove, and a pilot flickers under a gas-fed refrigerator. I have to step between piles of machine parts and tools, spread out on old newspapers messy with grease and mud.

"Fixing something?" I ask.

"Snowblower engine."

Reis wipes a hand across his mouth and waves to an empty kitchen chair for me to sit.

"It's what I do for a living," he says. "Fix things as broke for people. Something to drink?"

"No thank you."

"Afraid of my hospitality?"

"I don't want to put you to any trouble."

Reis scratches the jagged flap that remains of his right ear. I imagine this is the result of his last accident, when he went through his windshield. The ear looks chewed off.

"You always was the politest person I ever knowed," he says.

He turns away and reaches down a cup from a doorless cabinet, then pours out some coffee from a pot on the Coleman stove. He sets the cup in front of me, swipes his own off the table, and carries it back to the stove to refresh it.

"Matter of fact, I thought maybe you'd be too polite to come back," he says over his shoulder.

"I'm not staying for long."

Reis nods, and his hair flops in his eyes. It's darker now, not white blond.

"Na. Wouldn't think you would."

He rattles among empty food cartons, plates, glasses, and other trash on the counter, until he finds a pack of cigarettes. He holds it out to me.

"You smoke still?"

"I stopped two or three years after I left here."

"Me, too. Tried anyway. But I was in the prison a few times and ain't much to do there but smoke."

"So I've heard."

He spreads his mouth in something like a smile.

"About I was in the prison, or about smoking in prison?"

The scars on his face and hands, where the windshield had cut him, look less like things in themselves than blanks. The end of his cigarette glows vivid and red, momentarily the brightest spot in the room.

"Both," I reply.

I reach in my coat pocket and pull out an object wrapped in a handkerchief my grandmother had embroidered years ago.

"I don't know if you remember this," I say, setting it on the table. "I've carried it a long time. I even had it fixed. But it does belong to you. So."

Reis steps back to the table and pokes the handkerchief open, using the same hand in which he holds his cigarette. Smoke curls over the package. His hands, thick and splotched with grease, look clumsy, so the lightness of his touch comes as a surprise.

"Dainty stuff," he says, indicating the handkerchief. He picks up my gift and lets it hang between two fingers. "My daddy's good watch."

"Yes."

"I asked you to hold onto it."

"You don't want it?"

"Na, I'll take it back. Thank you. Thanks. Never know when something will come necessary."

He snatches it lightly into his shirt pocket and stubs out his cigarette among the half dozen or so other butts in the dented hubcap that serves as an ashtray.

He sits down across from me.

"Funny how when you're in jail you learn the value of things you ordinarily would take for granted," he says. "Trade there is the way, see. If you don't got nothin' to trade, you don't exist. So you better find something or invent it or steal it or you won't have enough of your guts left inside you by the end of a week to wish you was dead."

"I'm sorry you had to go through all that."

Reis looks at me uncomprehending for a moment.

"Were an old fellow in the same block as me the first time I was in," he says. "Drunk when they brung him in and stayed drunk two three days, there was that much in him, and only then did he start drying out. Went crazy shaking and seeing things as weren't really there and throwing up till he couldn't even dry heave no more. Didn't come in with nothin' on him and no one to bring him nothin' either. No cigarettes or comb or drugs or a few bucks. Were brought in for having relations with a cow. Which I guess the farmer what owned the cow didn't like any more than the cow."

He grins briefly and scratches his head.

"In the jail there was a guy called Bear. Big, ugly guy that you had to pay off before anybody else or you'd be sorry. He split with the guards, too, so there weren't no saving yourself by them. He'd get you alone and shake you down for whatever he wanted."

He lights another cigarette, tossing the match lightly into the hubcap on the table.

"That old fellow should of seen at least to arrange somebody to bring something into him to trade, but all he had was the clothes on his back that stank of puke and sweat and weren't even worth the wanting, so all he had really was his hair and his teeth. So when Bear got him alone in the toilet, it weren't even a case of shaking him down to find the most valuable thing. He just took his teeth. After that he were Bear's own, nobody else'd touch him."

He gives the hubcap a little spin that sends it sliding an inch or two away from him.

"Handier to fuck a mouth that got no teeth in it."

He picks up the embroidered handkerchief.

"This don't look like nothin', but you be surprised what it be worth in some corners. What something dainty as this could keep a person from having to give away. You sure you want to part with it?"

I gesture for him to keep it. He holds it up to the light and examines the lacy border.

"Your grandma were about the only person ever truly kind to me," he murmurs.

He settles into a thoughtful silence, and the light of the kerosene lamp momentarily resurrects in his expression the terrifying innocence I'd seen there long ago. Then he shifts a little and the look on his face passes, and it occurs to me that nothing I can do or say can possibly restore it.

I wonder how I ever thought I could.

Simple fear, most likely, or simple desire.

It's as hard to distinguish between those feelings now as it was when I was twelve, a boy slinking up the hill toward the barn, where Reis and I met in the dead of night when we were sure no one else would intrude. The fear of discovery had shaped the way we touched each other, the rhythm of our breathing, even the smells we inhaled—the pungent exhalations of old hay and sour beer left behind by other teenagers who used the barn for more or less the same purpose, though without the same need for stealth.

It was Toby Hewitt who told me that our secrecy was less than perfect. He came over one night toward the end of August, and we sat on the front porch drinking birch beer and talking about school, which was due to start up again in two weeks. We'd be entering eighth grade, the last year of junior high. And after that, we'd practically be adults.

Mosquitoes, drawn by the porch light, flew around our faces. Toby squashed one on his arm and it exploded blood, and then he told me everyone was saying Reis and I were queers. The word he used was *mos,* short for *homos.* Then he said he'd known me all his life, and he didn't think it was true.

"It's not true," I replied.

"I know it's not and you know it's not."

"What am I supposed to do, then?"

"You could talk to Dana and Charlie, I guess."

A dog trotted into the front yard then, a mutt with a white muzzle and missing part of an ear. It sat with its head cocked to one side watching us. When it understood that it wasn't going to get anything from us, it trotted back out to the road and down the hill, sniffing at bushes and clumps of grass along the way, leaving its mark in a few places. Coming unexpectedly on a candy wrapper, it stopped to lick whatever crumbs of chocolate still clung to the paper, and then continued on down the road, exploring.

"Guess I could talk to them," I said finally.

Toby swatted at another mosquito.

"Dana always said he was the one acted goofy."

I told Reis there wouldn't be anyone in the barn. It was Labor Day weekend, I said, and everyone who wasn't out of town would be down at Potter Lake to watch the fireworks. So I had to act suitably surprised when I saw Toby, Dana, and Charlie Holubeck inside, sitting on bales of old hay, smoking cigarettes and drinking cans of contraband beer.

The place stank unaccountably of cow dung, and the red light of sunset shone through cracks in the walls.

About a dozen boys in all had gathered there. Some were playing cards in an open space in the middle of the barn; the rest stood along the sides, or under the hayloft, where only the tips of their cigarettes sailing up and down in a weird ballet of orange coals proved them more than ghosts. Reis pulled up short at the door and glanced at me for a sign whether to stay or go.

I pretended to put a bold face on, and walked bravely inside calling, "Hey."

Toby came over and patted me on the back, an oddly formal gesture. He pushed a can of beer in my hand, then asked Reis if he wanted one. Reis stood right behind me, as if I were some type of shield, so Toby had to hand him a can of beer over my shoulder.

Then he invited us to sit, leading us to the circle of boys playing cards.

"Make a great clubhouse don't it?" Charlie said, when we sat down. "Don't know why we don't come here more frequent."

One of the boys looked up from the card game. His straight brown hair hung right in his face. " 'Cause it stinks," he said.

"So do you," Charlie replied.

Toby asked Reis if he'd ever come there much. Reis said no, not much. Then he pulled a wrinkled pack of Lucky Strikes from his shirt pocket and knocked one out for himself and one for me. I shook my head no and took another swallow of beer.

As Reis lit his cigarette, Kyle Gorman strolled out of the shadows and stood on the outer edge of the circle.

"Mind if have one of those?" he asked.

Reis flipped the pack across to him. Kyle turned it around and around in his hands, and asked Reis if he stole them. Reis replied he had his ways.

I remembered him saying the same thing when we were first getting to know each other. His cocksureness had impressed me then, his boldness.

I got up and walked to the back of the barn to look through the empty stalls. One of the boys standing back there nodded to me, and I recognized him as the one who had held me by the collar the day Kyle burned a scar in my palm.

"Well goodie for you-all," I heard Kyle say now, imitating Reis's accent.

There was laughter among the circle. I looked back to see Kyle light his cigarette and toss the pack back to Reis. Reis caught it in midair.

"Good-looking watch," Kyle said.

Reis shrugged. "Used to be my dad's."

"Steal that, too?"

I moved farther back in the stall and started pulling at a slat of rotting wood. I didn't hear how Reis replied, only Kyle asking him afterward if he stole a lot of stuff.

"Depends," Reis answered.

Another boy stepped into the circle and asked Reis what else he did. Reis replied, again, that it depended. From where I was standing, I could see him crane his neck, looking for me; but he couldn't see me. A moment later, he stood up to leave.

"Hey sit down, Reis," Charlie told him. "We can go over my house later and play some pool in the basement."

"That something you like to do?" Kyle asked. "Shoot pool?"

"Maybe he likes the basement," someone else said.

"Maybe he likes the shape of the stick."

Reis began to edge away from the circle of boys. Though he still couldn't see me, he called, "Hey Chris, you want to go?"

"Hey Chris," Kyle said. "You-all wanna 'mo?"

There was more laughter now. I watched Reis turn around and see the entrance to the barn cut off by another boy, as Kyle started walking toward him.

"You-all a 'mo?" he asked.

Reis shook his head.

"You tried to 'mo Dana down in his basement last year," Charlie shouted.

"That's a goddamned lie!" Reis shouted back. "He tried it on me."

Kyle turned to Dana, who was sitting very still on a bale of hay.

"That true?" he asked.

"No," Dana replied. "He tried to kiss my dick."

Reis looked around once more for me and called out, asking if I was ready to go.

"Okay," Toby said, and in twos and threes, the boys stood and formed a kind of circle around Reis.

"Come on kiss me homo," Kyle said.

Abruptly, the circle broke apart as Reis jumped, not backward but inward, kicking at the boys closest to him and smashing with his fists. Charlie went down, and after him, someone else. Toby hopped around the perimeter of the group, yelling.

The fight lasted less than five minutes and ended as suddenly as it had started. The clump of boys moved back, silently, and I could see from between their bodies that Reis was standing in the middle of the circle. His shirt was torn and a spill of blood oozed from his nose. Kyle stood facing him, a switchblade balanced in his outstretched hand.

Kyle lunged, and each time, Reis jumped out of the way, inching backward until he came close enough to one of the other boys, who stuck out his leg and tripped him. A ragged cheer rose as Reis fell to the ground. Then Kyle jumped on him and dragged him back to standing, twisting one of his arms behind his back and holding the switchblade to his neck. He looked around for Dana, who stood on the outer edge of the circle, rubbing his chin where Reis had punched him.

"Pulaski, you try something on this kid?" Kyle asked.

"Nope," Dana replied.

"Think he ought to be going around spreading trash about you?"

"Nope."

"Hm," Kyle said. "Maybe you better put a stop to it, then."

Dana walked over to Reis and punched him hard in the stomach. Reis doubled over.

"Liar," he breathed.

Kyle shook his head. "Says you a liar, Pulaski."

Then Dana kicked Reis in the groin. Reis went all the way down, and Kyle let him fall in the dirt. After a minute, he struggled to all fours and crawled away from the circle, retching. Then he sagged to the ground in fetal position, holding his wrist and rubbing it, as if he'd sprained it or broken it, falling. Kyle followed and stood over him.

"Who's the liar, kid?"

Silence.

"You or Pulaski?"

More silence.

"Stop it," I said, stepping from the shadows.

"Don't stick up for him Chris," Toby said. "He's a damn homo."

Just then, Reis lashed up with his hand. He'd slipped his watch off and seemed to be trying to use the metal band to cut Kyle's face. Kyle caught his fist easily enough, though, and squeezed down hard. Reis screamed, a high-pitched, terrible sound. I thought I could hear bones cracking.

I stepped all the way out of the stall, screaming at Kyle to stop.

He didn't pay any attention, but instead pulled Reis up by the arm and began dragging him toward the stalls. As they drew past I begged Kyle to please stop. He looked me up and down, grinning so the scar under his eye folded and unfolded like a lightning bolt. Then he spat a tiny piece of something in the dirt, and tugged at Reis and asked him if he was coming. Reis allowed himself to be dragged along.

He balked at the entrance, though, and Kyle had to call one of the other boys to help. At that moment, Reis twisted his hand free and dropped his father's watch at my feet.

"Hold on to it for me," he whispered thickly.

Then the other boy came up and pushed Reis from behind into the stall. I bent down to pick up the watch, and as I stood up again, I caught sight of Kyle shoving down Reis's pants and underpants and pressing him down to the dirt floor. Then he undid his own pants and was beginning to lower himself on top of Reis when his helper pushed the stall door closed and there was nothing else to see.

I turned and saw the others coming together in the gloom, collecting their beer cans and cigarettes and playing cards. Someone lit a cigarette, letting the match fall on a bale of hay. Instantly, another boy scuffed at it with his heel, whispering an angry *Jesus*.

I didn't move until the first cry sounded from behind the stall door, and then abruptly I was outside, running down the hill. Away from the barn, anywhere, into the meadow below.

I stopped when I got to the creek, and sat on the rocks, clutching the gold watch. The crystal was cracked and the two hands were twisted, but it continued to beat in my hand like the heart of a living thing.

At one point, I thought I heard a rustling behind me, which might have been the wind, or another person, or even an animal. I wasn't interested enough to be afraid, however.

I sat a long while before going back to the barn.

I stopped just outside the door to listen, then stepped inside and called Reis's name a couple of times. I kicked at one of the bales of hay until it came apart, and then I noticed a pack of matches someone had left behind. I picked it up and lit one after another until they were all gone, the last whole action I performed for many years.

As I came down the hill, all the other houses were dark except my grandmother's. I closed the kitchen door softly behind me when I stepped inside, though I knew there wasn't much point to it. My grandmother stepped almost immediately into the kitchen, dressed in the same cotton nightgown she always wore at night, her hair hanging in a braid down her back.

She asked if I knew what time it was, and I replied that I didn't. She said it was after one o'clock in the morning, and she was just about to call the sheriff. All I could think to say was that I was sorry.

Then she asked where I'd been all night.

"Out," I replied.

"Where?"

"Just out. Around."

She stared at me, hard. "Drinking?"

"No."

But she continued to stare, so I told her I'd had two beers with Dana and Toby.

"I called over to Hewitt's," she said. "The mother said she hadn't seen you. I called Pulaski's, too."

"We went to the schoolyard."

"It closes nine o'clock."

"I guess we kind of wandered after that."

She shook her head. "I don't see why you couldn't come right home, instead of letting me go crazy worrying about you half the night."

I wanted to step into her arms and have her hold me. To amaze her with my ability to read. To sit by the rocks and listen to her stories.

"I'm sorry," I replied. "I won't do it again."

I noticed a spool of adhesive tape on the kitchen table, and next to it, a pair of scissors. I picked up the scissors, absent-mindedly, then looked across at my grandmother standing in the doorway, arms folded across her chest.

"You have to stay on couch tonight," she said. "Or make up your ma's old bed. I don't got the strength do it myself."

"What's wrong with my room?"

"Reis is up there."

She waited.

"Some bad boys got at him tonight," she said. "His ma is to work and he were scared to go home."

"Is he hurt?"

She breathed in and out. "What was you doing with Dana and Toby?"

Slowly, I returned the scissors to the table.

"Nothing," I replied.

My grandmother took a step into the kitchen, and raised her arm. I backed away toward the kitchen door; and in the same instant, she sagged against the wall, shaking her head slowly back and forth. I thought she might cry. Instead, she turned around to go to her room.

Halfway through the door, she stopped and looked at me.

"Thought I brung you up better than that," she said.

The mattress in my mother's old room was lumpy, and stank of alcohol and sickness. Desperately, I prayed for the sickness to enter my body and make me die then and there, though I was no longer sure who I was praying to or if anyone could hear me.

It seemed impossible I'd ever fall asleep, and when at last I did, my dreams were full of jangling sounds and people shouting.

I woke up just before dawn to find my grandmother at the window, staring through the backyard up the hill. I thought I smelled fireplace smoke, which didn't make any sense, since it was summer. Between the smell and the way my grandmother stood unmoving at the window, I thought I might still be dreaming.

She heard me stirring and turned around. Then I saw she wasn't a dream; she had a human face after all, though flickering with a strange light.

She let the curtain fall.

"Barn's on fire," she said, and walked past me out the bedroom door.

Reis avoids my eyes, standing and shuffling back through the debris on the kitchen floor to the counter where he'd left his cup. Huge shadows cast by the kerosene lamp stalk him across the walls. He looks down at his rough boots, his botched knees.

"Except the prison," he says, "I ain't been out from around here since I come up from Alabama. More than twenty years now. I expect it's an interesting place out there. Got to be more interesting than here."

"Come for a visit and see."

"Ya." He laughs shortly.

I sit a moment longer and then slide out of my chair and step across to him until we're standing barely an inch apart. I raise my hand and bring the tips of my fingers to rest on his cheek. Reis stands limply, as if inertia might deflect my touch, while I explore the muscles of his face, the delicate closed eyelids.

"I want to do the right thing by you," I whisper.

Reis opens his eyes, pale green still, the color of dry grass. "Don't see the use of it, little brother."

I don't move or flinch. "What can I do? What can I say?"

"You don't need me to tell you."

"Please. I do."

"Huh."

Reis pushes his toe against a spilled jar of screws on the floor until he just about has it righted; then he lets it fall again.

"Seems you come a long way for nothin' then."

For a second, I almost laugh. Whatever hope or desire I may have harbored suddenly snaps shut, and I drop my hands, clasping them in front of me like a penitent.

Here is the real loss: not in the past, but in the present.

I was prepared for anger.

I was prepared for violence.

"I don't forgive you," Reis says simply. "I don't not forgive you, either. But I don't forgive you."

It takes three days to finish cleaning out my grandmother's house. On the last day, I wake up early, thinking I hear a noise downstairs. Which is impossible, I tell myself.

The house is virtually empty; even the rugs have been rolled up, waiting for the Salvation Army trucks to take them away, along with the rest of the furniture and some boxes full of clothes and other odds and ends. Emptiness amplifies every sound. When I'd called New York to let Richard know my flight times, my voice sounded hollow, as if I were speaking in a cavern.

Then I hear the noise again.

I slip into my pants and shirt, and step cautiously to the head of the stairs. I'm not sure what I'll do if there's an intruder. Anything I could use to defend myself has been packed up or thrown away.

I call out, then wait for a response. I call again.

There's no sign of an intruder downstairs. I can't be sure, of course, since everything but the furniture is boxed up: What would seem out of place? Still, the doors are closed and locked from the inside, and so are the windows, and I don't see any tracks on the floor. So my first instinct was right, I think, standing in the kitchen now: It was just the house settling.

Then I smell something, which isn't as easy to explain.

I smell bread.

There must be a cause, something I've forgotten in the cupboards or the refrigerator, maybe even something that's fallen behind the stove. It could be a combination of things. Or, it could simply be the way the house smells now that everything else has been stripped away.

Still, it brings me back to unfinished business; and as I stand at the kitchen window looking out at the morning shining back at itself in muddy puddles in the front yard and the road beyond, it occurs to me that I know how to finish it.

At 9:20, the Salvation Army truck rolls up in front of the house. Two young men with round, bearded faces load out the beds, the dressers, tables, chairs, and boxes. They're very efficient. They call me *sir,* and I wonder if I will continue to find this disturbing.

Maybe not. A part of me looks forward to a crotchety old age: frightening small children with my frown lines and goopy eyes, harassing bus drivers, loudly demanding to talk to store managers.

I think it will be a nice change, finally, to be on the side that's scary.

The man who rents us his boat thinks that Judith and I are crazy to go out on the lake in the winter. His opinion isn't improved when he finds out what we're going to do once we're out there. In his opinion—which is not invited, but offered nonetheless—people should be buried in the ground. Of course, this does not keep him from accepting money for the use of his boat.

Judith and I face each other on rough wooden planks that serve as seats. She holds the box of ashes on her lap, while I row. The hills on either side of the lake gradually close around us, and when we reach what looks like the middle, I pull the oars in and lock them into place along the rim. Judith hands the box across to me and I pry up the lid. It comes off with a muffled pop.

The ashes surprise me. I've imagined them pale and dry, like powder; but they're more like gray clumps mixed with chunks of bone, one of which is easily as long as my finger. When I dip my hand in I can feel their heaviness. And the horror, too, of holding the insides of someone I loved.

How long ago that seems now, irredeemably long.

I shiver, but not from cold.

The wind tears at the ashes in my hand, and I hastily dump them over the water. They don't sink, but float on top of the waves, like dust. I offer the box to Judith.

"No," she says. "You finish it."

From under her coat she pulls a Bible. Something ought to be read, she says, unless I object. I don't, so she opens the book and smooths the pages and starts to read, her voice reedy but distinct. The boat rocks up and down, a trail of ashes fanning wider and wider behind it, drifting away.

"*And Sarah died in Kirjatharba,*" she reads, "*the same is Hebron in the land of Canaan: and Abraham came to mourn for Sarah, and to weep for her. And Abraham stood up from before his dead, and spake unto the sons of Heth, saying I am a stranger and a sojourner with you: give me possession of a burying place with you, that I may bury my dead out of my sight.*

"*And the Children of Heth answered Abraham, saying unto him, Hear us, my lord: thou art a mighty prince among us: in the choice of our sepulchers bury thy dead; none of us shall withhold from thee his sepulcher, but that thou mayst bury thy dead.*

"*And Abraham stood up, and bowed himself to the people of the land, even to the children of Heth. And he communed with them, saying, If it be your mind that I should bury my dead out of my sight, hear me, and entreat for me to Ephron the son of Zohar, that he may give me the cave of Machpelah, which he hath, which is in the end of his field; for as much money as it is worth he shall give it me for a possession of a burying place among you.*"

Judith closes the book and hugs it to her chest.

"Strange," she says. "I don't feel like crying."

"I think she'd like knowing she's buried here."

"So do I."

"I think it makes sense."

"Yes it does."

A gull sweeps past overhead. We shade our eyes against the sun and watch it circle a few times and then head for the opposite shore.

Maybe it's the gull that makes me think of the times my grandmother stood on the front porch, waiting for me to come back from school. I wonder if she waited for Reis after he moved in with her. If she walked with him down to the meadow and sat on the rocks, watching the creek flow past. Or did she walk alone, looking for some sign of all the people who had passed?

"It's crossed my mind," I say after a while, "not to sell the house at all. That I should hang onto it, use it as a vacation place, maybe. A retreat. I suppose I could even rent it out."

Judith smiles, but I can see the idea makes her uneasy.

"It was just a thought," I add. "More sentimental than practical."

"I don't see why you would." She corrects herself. "Would want to, I mean."

The wind picks up, setting waves in motion, rocking the boat. Judith wraps her coat more tightly around herself, and I remember how thin she is now, and that we're both at an age where cold is beginning to matter a bit more than when we were young. I release the oars and start to row back to the dock.

"It's easier to think of you far away," Judith says.

"Out of sight, out of mind."

"Oh no, never out of mind. It's just that, for better or worse, I've made my place here. I know the terrain."

She turns and looks out over the water.

I remain silent, watching her face, memorizing it. I don't pay enough attention to those kinds of details.

After a moment, I tell her I understand.

"I had a patient not too long ago," I explain. "A boy of sixteen who actually wanted to move in with me. He thought I'd want him as a lover."

"What did you say to that?"

"I told him no, of course. For all the ethical reasons. It would have been wrong."

The dock comes into view now, and I can see the man who owns the boat coming down from his house. I wonder if he's been watching the whole time, waiting for something awful to happen, which would justify his bad opinion of us; I wonder if he's disappointed to see that we've come safely back to shore.

"Actually, I told him I wasn't gay."

The man on the dock waves. Maybe he's relieved to see us back safe and sound.

He reaches out a boat hook.

Just a few more strokes before he pulls us in.

An alarm sounds as I go through the metal detector at the Columbus airport, and the guard tells me nonchalantly to empty my pockets, placing my keys, change, and any other metal objects into a plastic dish. Although I understand the need, I find the extra measure of precaution frustrating because I'm running late and my plane is already boarding.

When I pass through the detector a second time, I'm certified safe. Hurriedly, I swipe up the things I dumped in the plastic dish and head down toward the gate.

"Sir?" the guard calls after me.

When I turn, I see he's holding up a thin gold medallion.

"I think you forgot this," he says.

I return to where he's standing and thank him.

"It was my grandmother's," I explain.

He's studying the back of the medallion.

"The writing," he says. "It's Polish."

"You can read it?" I ask.

He nods. "Anna Mickiewicz, First Holy Communion," he reads. He smiles broadly as he hands me the medallion. It's a nice smile, with a wide gap between the two front teeth. A smile you could trust.

"That was your grandmother, Anna Mickiewicz?"

I consider saying yes; it's a small thing, after all, and easier than trying to explain. Instead, I shake my head.

"I have no idea who she was."

The last of the passengers has already boarded when I reach the gate. The attendant tells me not to worry, people are still finding their seats, so the plane won't move for another five minutes at least. She checks my seat assignment and tears out a piece of my ticket. As she hands me my boarding pass, she wishes me a pleasant flight.

Even though I know there's no need to rush, I still walk at a brisk clip through the gateway. I don't like tunnels of any kind, really. I can't help thinking they're going to collapse or explode, that the air is full of poisons. But at least this one's short, and as the little knot of passengers ahead clears the door and moves inside the plane, there is an instant of light.

Eric Swanson was educated at Yale University and the Juilliard School. His first novel, *The Greenhouse Effect*, was published in 1990. More recently, he has written two guides on animal care, as well as *Hero Cats*, a collection of stories about altruistic behavior among felines. His short work has appeared in *Christopher Street, Body Positive*, and *Family Circle*.